Weird Science

Suddenly there was a flash of blinding light and an ear-piercing blast of white noise. I closed my eyes, covered my ears, and fell back onto the rug. Then the room fell silent and I heard the aliens gasp.

I opened my eyes and crawled to my knees. What I saw was almost too much for my tiny Earth brain to comprehend. Captain Spotless, Lady Bug, Chauncy, and four tiny Stickky Elves were standing in front of the televisions. They weren't two-dimensional cartoons, and they weren't 3-D computer simulations either. They were real.

Neighbors from Outer Space

Neighbors from Outer Space

Francess Lantz

Rainbow Bridge®

Troll

Published by Rainbow Bridge, an imprint and trademark of
Troll Communications L.L.C.

Printed in the United States of America.

10 9 8 7 6 5 4

For Preston

And with thanks to John Landsberg, Ellen Jackson, Lou Lynda Richards, and Mary Smith for their out-of-this-world support.

≫ Chapter ≪

1

I guess I should have realized right away our new neighbors were going to be different. After all, the moving van that delivered their furniture had these words on the side: Intergalactic Movers—Across the U.S. or Across the Universe.

"Pretty catchy motto, eh, Russell?" my father said as we stood together at the window. Dad works for an advertising agency. He spends his days thinking up exciting new ways to sell tuna fish and blue jeans and plastic garbage bags. He's good at it, too. Last year he was Uniglobe Advertising Agency's Man of the Year.

I flopped onto the couch and went back to watching the baseball game on our big-screen TV. "Have you seen this new commercial?" I asked, pointing at the screen. "The polar bear morphs into a refrigerator. It's awesome."

"Hrmph," Dad grumbled. "That's an Adworld International commercial. Our competitors."

"Oops, sorry. Actually, the computer animation isn't half

as good as the Zipsi-Cola ad you did. Remember, the one with the hula-dancing soda cans?"

Dad's face broke into a grin. "One of my masterpieces, if I do say so myself."

"I wonder if the new neighbors have any children," my mother said, walking in from the kitchen and joining Dad at the window.

Dad peered through the miniblinds. "That would be nice," he agreed. "Maybe someone Russell's age."

Lately my parents had started bugging me to make new friends. According to them, I spent too much time in front of the television set. "I *have* a friend," I muttered, moving a little closer to the screen. "Travis."

"But all you two ever do is watch TV," my mother said.

"That's not true. We collect TV trading cards, and we're writing our own TV commercial trivia book." I hopped up from the couch. "Here's a question for you. In the original 1957 Radoline Motor Oil ad, what was the name of the Radoline rabbit?"

"Wait, I know that one," Dad said, scrunching up his forehead in concentration. Suddenly his face brightened. "Raddy Rabbit! Later renamed Rad Rabbit when they brought him back during the 1989 ad campaign."

"Way to go, Dad!" I exclaimed. We exchanged a grin and slapped a high five. Mom watched us and smiled proudly.

I guess I should explain right now about my family. Sure, Mom and Dad worry once in a while that I don't spend enough time out in the fresh air. But the truth is, my entire family lives for television. Or, to be more precise, television commercials.

You see, it's part of my dad's job to watch all the new

commercials. And since my mom is a TV commercial actress (you probably remember her from that famous aspirin commercial—the one where the lady says, "It feels like my head is caught in an enormous steel mousetrap!") she watches them, too.

My parents also get a lot of free products from the companies they work for. For example, right now my dad is working on the Sunlight Tuna account, which means we've been eating a lot of tuna casserole. We also get plenty of free promotional merchandise—stuff like mugs with the Big Mouth Bubblegum logo on the side, Zipsi-Cola T-shirts, even a telephone in the shape of a Sunlight tuna.

Naturally, all this had a big effect on me when I was growing up. While other little boys dreamed of being Superman or a Teenage Mutant Ninja Turtle, I dreamed of being Captain Spotless, the cartoon superhero from the Spotless Cleanser commercials. Captain Spotless was big and strong, and he flew around killing germs with his superpowered soap bubbles. Besides, I liked his gold tooth.

My other heroes were Chauncy, the cartoon dog from the Prime Cut Dog Food commercials, and Lady Bug, the animated half-insect, half-woman hero of the BugBeGone Bug Spray ads. And then there were the Stickky Elves—Bo, Bill, Bert, and Binky—those little cartoon creatures that wrapped packages "in the blink of an eye" in the Stickky Adhesive Tape commercials. For a long time I didn't believe in Santa Claus. I thought the Stickky Elves delivered all the Christmas presents.

Of course, that was years ago. By the time the new neighbors moved in, I knew perfectly well that commercials were created to sell stuff, and characters like Chauncy and the Stickky Elves were thought up by advertising executives like my dad to make money.

Still, Captain Spotless and his cohorts were like friends I had grown up with. When I was little I used to pretend I was traveling through the television with them, ridding the world of evil. Sometimes I still dream about it. I know it sounds silly, but in my dreams Captain Spotless, Chauncy, Lady Bug, and the Stickky Elves seem more real than anyone I've known in my regular life. I guess that's why deep down—although I would never tell this to anyone, not even Travis—I sometimes find myself wishing that they really existed.

My mother's voice cut into my daydream like a knife sliding through Sunny Day Margarine. "I don't see any kid stuff coming out of the moving van," she said. "No bikes or basketball hoops or anything."

Dad squinted into the sunlight. "The only thing I've seen so far are TVs."

"TVs?" I repeated, perking up.

"Yep. They've unloaded about ten of them so far."

Mom shook her head. "And I thought we watched a lot of television. These people must be boob-tube addicts!"

I walked to the window and peered across the yard. The movers were heaving television set after television set out of the van and lugging them into the house. In the next five minutes, we counted six 27-inch sets, twelve 19-inch sets, and fourteen of those little mini-TVs you can set up in the bathroom.

"The new neighbors must own a TV store," Dad said.

"Or a repair shop," Mom suggested.

"Out of their house?" I asked.

"Seems unlikely," Dad admitted. "Still, no normal family would own that many televisions just for their own enjoyment."

Dad was right. We only owned four TVs, and we were professionals. I frowned and bit my lip. I was starting to get the feeling our new neighbors were no normal family. Still, I never expected they'd be from outer space.

The morning after the new neighbors moved in, I was sitting in the living room watching a *Beverly Hillbillies* rerun. Dad was at work, of course. He usually leaves the house at about seven A.M. and gets home around eight, if it's not a busy day. I miss him, but as he points out, he didn't get to be Uniglobe's Man of the Year by sitting on his duff.

I was jotting down a few notes for my TV commercial trivia book when Mom walked into the room with a plate of granola chocolate chip cookies.

"Thanks, Mom," I said. "I'm starving."

"They're not for you," she replied. "They're for the new neighbors. I want you to go next door and say hello."

To tell you the truth, I had pretty much forgotten about the new family next door. Sure, I was curious about why they had so many TVs. In fact, last night before I fell asleep I had found myself wondering if there might be a kid living there who was as obsessed by television as I was—a new friend maybe, someone to trade *Batman* and *Star Trek* cards with.

But by morning, the possibility had seemed pretty unlikely. Probably Mom and Dad were right—the new neighbors owned a television repair shop. Either that or they were a family of weirdos—the kind of people who

13

think aliens talk to them through their TV sets or something goofy like that.

"Why do *I* have to go next door?" I asked.

"Because your father's at work and I'm late. I'm shooting a hair spray commercial at eleven o'clock."

"But Uniglobe's new deodorant commercial is premiering today. I promised Dad I'd watch it."

"You can see it tonight, hon." She grabbed her purse and headed out the door. "I left a few cookies in the kitchen for you to eat when you get back. Have a good day."

The door closed and I was alone in the cool, dark house. We always lower the miniblinds during the day to keep the glare off the TV screens. I watched the rest of *The Beverly Hillbillies* and waited for Dad's commercial, but it didn't appear. I knew I should go next door, but I hated the thought of going outside into the hot, bright sunshine.

I thought of Travis, away at survival camp in Oregon for the entire month. His parents had forced him to go. His dad said he was turning into a pasty wimp and he needed to get sunburn on his nose and calluses on his hands. Poor Travis. There probably wasn't a television set within twenty miles of Camp Sink or Swim.

I watched an *Andy Griffith Show* rerun and then decided I'd better go next door before my mom came home and yelled at me. I picked up the cookies and walked outside, squinting down at the blazing white sidewalk. Immediately I began to sweat, and not just because of the heat.

The truth is, I'm kind of an introvert—at least that's what my sixth-grade teacher wrote on my report card at the end of last year. I mean, I'm totally relaxed around my parents, and talking to Travis is a cinch. But when it comes to

14

introducing myself to strangers—well, let's just say my armpits were doing a terrific impression of Niagara Falls.

I dragged my feet across the lawn and rang the new neighbors' doorbell. While I waited, I shifted from foot to foot and gazed up and down the street. Ours is a typical Southern California neighborhood. White houses with red tile roofs, grass so green it looks as if it came from an Easter basket, skinny palm trees swaying overhead. Just like television, only *real*—which means a lot less safe and predictable.

I counted to ten, then back to one. Good. Nobody home. I turned, ready to hightail it back to my comfortable television set, when the door opened and there they were— the new neighbors.

There were two grown-ups and a boy about my age. They were tall and slender, with moon-shaped faces and pale bluish-white skin. All three of them were wearing matching red-and-purple jogging suits and multicolored athletic shoes. I looked past them into the living room. A huge multilevel shelving unit stood against the far wall—the kind of thing people use to store their TV, VCR, and stereo, plus videotapes, books, and records. But these shelves held nothing except TV sets. There must have been two dozen of them.

"Uh . . . uh . . . welcome to the neighborhood," I mumbled. "My name is Russell Brinkerhoff and I live next—"

"Oh, cookies!" the woman squealed. "Wholesome and delicious!"

"Just like Grandma used to make," the man chimed in. "But even better because they're available at your local supermarket."

15

"N-no, they aren't," I stammered. "My mom made these."

"Um-um, good!" the boy shouted. He grabbed a cookie and took a big bite. Then he turned and spit the whole mouthful on the floor!

"Hey!" I cried.

"No, no!" the man scolded. "Mom just waxed that floor, and my boss is coming over for dinner."

"Don't worry, dear," the woman said. "Spills and stains wipe away in a snap with Mop-N-Shine."

Then they all started to sing: "Mop-N-Shine, Mop-N-Shine, saves you money, saves you time!"

"Well, uh . . . I gotta go," I said, backing down the porch steps.

"Don't leave," the kid cried. "I've got sixteen televisions in my room, and I know the words to every dog food commercial!"

I turned and ran.

Chapter

2

id the new neighbors seem friendly?" Mom asked when she came home that afternoon.

"Oh, yeah, sure," I said. I was afraid if I told her the truth she'd think I'd gone bonkers. As a matter of fact, I was beginning to wonder if I hadn't. I mean, were those people next door for real or had I fallen asleep in front of the TV and dreamed them? I wasn't completely sure.

"What did they look like?" Mom asked.

"You know . . . ordinary."

"So what's with all those TVs? Did you find out?"

"Not really," I said. "I, uh . . . I didn't stick around to ask."

"Well, we don't want to be nosy." She smiled. "Are there any kids your age?"

"I guess so. I mean, there's a boy."

"Good for you," she said enthusiastically. "Does he seem nice?"

I shrugged. "I think he's allergic to cookies."

That night I couldn't sleep. I kept thinking about the new neighbors. I was pretty certain I hadn't dreamed them— even *I* couldn't come up with a dream that freaky. But if they were real, then that meant I might actually have to talk to them again. For some reason, the thought sent an icy chill down my spine.

I suppose I should have been thrilled to meet a family that was even more enthusiastic about TV than I was. But I couldn't help thinking there was something weird about them—besides the fact that they acted like a bunch of living, breathing television commercials, I mean. That kid had sort of purple eyes. And that bump in his hair didn't look like a cowlick.

The next morning, I found myself peering out the window at their house. My dad had brought home a videotape of the commercials that were nominated for this year's Clio awards—the Oscar of the advertising industry—but I couldn't concentrate on it. I kept thinking about the new neighbors. Their living room had looked awfully bare. Come to think of it, I hadn't seen anything except televisions. No sofa, no chairs, nothing. Didn't they ever sit down?

But the really strange thing was, although part of me felt totally weirded out by these people, part of me was sort of attracted to them. All day long I found myself thinking about them, wondering if they knew the words to all the Stickky Tape commercials, and if the kid loved Captain Spotless as much as I did.

That night, I lay awake thinking about the people next door. I had to find out more about them. But no way was I going to ring their doorbell again. For one thing, how did I know these people weren't lunatics who kidnapped young neighbor children, chopped their bodies into little pieces, and stuffed them in the back of their TV sets? For another thing, I was just too shy.

That left only one possibility—I would sneak next door and spy on them, preferably under cover of night. Like, for example, right now.

I got out of bed, pulled a pair of jeans over my pajamas, and climbed out my bedroom window. The moon was full and a hot wind was making the palm trees bend and rattle. Slowly, silently, like Lady Bug sneaking up on a kitchen full of roaches, I tiptoed next door. Then I crawled through the bushes beside the back door and peeked in the window.

The new kid was sitting on the floor, staring at a row of sixteen televisions. "Seven hundred sheets in every roll of Whisper Soft Toilet Tissue," he said along with the lady on the TVs. "Now that's what I call a bargain!"

Even from the back, he looked a little odd. His head was as round as the full moon that was shining up in the sky. And then there was that odd bump under his hair, and his blindingly bright pink-and-black jogging suit.

The commercial ended and one for Sunlight Tuna came on. "From the sun-dappled seas where dolphins roam, we bring our tuna to your home," he crooned along with the voice on the television.

The kid rolled onto his side and I caught a glimpse of his feet. I felt my mouth fall open. They were as big as my dad's, and the toes looked like my fingers. "This is getting really bizarre," I murmured.

Just then, the commercial ended and a cartoon came on. The kid pointed his little finger at the TV. Suddenly, the channel changed, just as if he was using a remote control!

"Yikes!" I gasped. I leaped backward, ready to retreat to the safety of my own relatively normal family, but there was a bush in my way. A bush covered with prickly thorns. "Ow!" I yelped, staggering forward. I tripped over a fallen palm frond and fell headfirst into the windowpane.

The kid heard the thump and froze. I stared at him, my knees in the dirt and my cheek pressed against the glass, too petrified to move. Slowly he turned around and saw me. I tried to run, but my feet seemed to have grown roots.

The kid got up, walked to the window, and opened it. He was staring right at me with his sort of purple eyes.

"Don't suck out my brain!" I begged. "I won't tell anyone what I saw!"

"Tell a neighbor! Tell a friend!" he said. "Our new frequent caller program can save you money!" He grinned and reached out to touch my arm.

"Don't vaporize me!" I shrieked.

Suddenly, the kid looked worried. "What are you talking about?" he asked. "Why would I do that?"

"Because . . . because I saw you change the channels with your finger."

The grin came back. "Now you, too, can have the wisdom of the ages at *your* fingertips," he said. "Just dial 1-900-PSYCHIC."

"Will you stop that!" I shouted.

The kid frowned. "What's wrong?"

"What's wrong?" I repeated. "You keep talking like a TV commercial. You've got purple eyes, ape feet, and a strange bump on your head. And you change channels with your finger!"

"Well, how do *you* do it?" he asked.

"With a remote control."

"Oh, man, I knew it," he groaned. "I told the X-10 underground we'd never pass as humans. I just didn't think we'd blow our cover so soon."

"You mean you're . . . you're . . ." I stammered.

"An alien," he said with a nod.

Chapter

3

*A*liens! My new next-door neighbors were aliens. I tried to scream, but it came out sounding like a pathetic little whine.

"Pl-pl-please," I stammered, "don't do it. We're just a boring, unimportant little planet. We're not even worth invading."

"Invading?" He chuckled. "I wouldn't know where to start. Listen, just promise me you won't tell anyone about us. We're supposed to be undercover."

"But why?" I whimpered. "What do you want with us?"

"Look, Russell," he said, "why don't you come inside and I'll explain everything."

"How do you know my name?" I whined. "Did you read my mind?"

"Don't be silly. You told me yesterday."

"Oh, yeah." I stood there, trying to make sense of what was happening. Okay, so my new neighbors were from outer space. Fine. The real question was this: Were they the

E.T. kind of aliens, or the *Invasion of the Body Snatchers* kind? In other words, were they going to unlock the secrets of the universe for me or were they planning to turn me into a drooling, brain-dead zombie? I looked into the kid's pale, moon-shaped face. He didn't look very threatening.

"Oh, come on," he said. "We can watch some commercials together. I'll even show you how I change channels with my finger."

"Well . . . okay. Just promise you won't suck out my brain."

"Like a promise from a close friend," he said reassuringly. "You can count on Madison Life Insurance to be there when you aren't."

He reached out a pale, slender hand to me. I hesitated, then grabbed it and let him pull me in the window.

"Welcome to my hut," my new neighbor said, gesturing around the room. "My name is Minivan."

"I beg your pardon?"

"Minivan. My parents named me after their favorite flashie." He pretended he was steering a car and began babbling something that sounded like Japanese.

"Is that your native language?" I asked with awe.

"Don't be silly," he said. "That's Japanese. My parents' favorite flashie is about a Japanese family buying a new car."

"Oh," I squeaked, too freaked out to bother asking why he called TV commercials "flashies."

"My native language sounds completely different," he continued. "For example, my last name is . . ."

He pursed his lips and let out a noise that sounded like a loud sneeze with a burp at the end.

"Wow!"

"How about you?" he asked. "Were you named after a flashie?"

"No, I was named after my great-uncle on my mother's side. Listen," I said nervously, "I don't mean to pry but, uh . . . where exactly do you come from? And what are you doing here on Earth?"

"It's top secret. You can't tell anyone, or else."

"Or else what?" I asked anxiously.

"Or else they'll find out." Now it was his turn to look anxious. "And then they might hurt us. You're not going to hurt us, are you, Russell?"

I couldn't believe it. Minivan seemed even more frightened of me than I was of him. I smiled. I was really starting to like this guy. I decided to quote from a TV commercial to make him feel at ease. "One squirt of Hanson and Hanson First-Aid Spray and the hurt is all gone," I said, imitating the mother in the commercial.

Minivan picked up the reference immediately. "I love you, Mommy," he cooed, pretending to be the little girl.

We looked at each other and burst out laughing. Part of me was in shock—I mean, this was an alien I was joking around with. But part of me felt as relaxed and comfortable as if I was fooling around with Travis.

"Sit down, Russell," Minivan said, still smiling. "I'll explain everything."

"Okay." I sat down cross-legged on the rug. Then Minivan sat, and my eyes bugged out. He was sitting as if there was a chair under him, looking perfectly comfortable. The only problem was there was no chair in sight—his butt was resting in midair!

I learned a lot about Minivan that evening. He and his folks came from the planet Xarabibble-10 (X-10 for short). If you go to Jupiter and turn left, X-10 is about five hundred light-years away, give or take a light-minute. According to Minivan, X-10 is the most boring planet in the entire universe—or at least it was until they discovered TV commercials.

It seems the Xarabibblian chief was sitting around one day, trying to figure out how to use the new faster-than-light transgalactic audiovisual receiver that his neighbors from Xarabibble-6 had just given him, when all of a sudden he picked up these amazing transmissions. Turns out they were TV commercials from Planet Earth, but he didn't know that at first. All he knew was that the transmissions were loud and colorful and exciting, and they showed a world full of happy creatures who liked to sing, dance, and wear athletic clothing.

The chief bought more audiovisual receivers from the X-6 scientists. Then he gave them to the Xarabibblians so they could all watch the commercials—or flashies, as he called them. In return, everyone had to pay the government a monthly fee.

Before long, the whole planet was wild about flashies. They watched them day and night, and they learned how to speak English and a dozen other Earth languages in the process. They even tried to act like them—which explained why Minivan and his parents had recited commercials to me yesterday.

"But what about the TV shows?" I said. "Don't you watch those, too?"

"What are TV shows?" Minivan asked.

"You know, the stuff between the commercials." I pointed to the sixteen TVs, which were showing a hospital drama. "Like this."

He frowned. "On X-10 the only thing between the commercials is static," he said.

"Weird," I said.

Minivan glanced at the hospital drama. "I don't know what this stuff is, but it's not as much fun as commercials. Where are the bright colors, the fast action, the happy people? These people look very depressed."

I had to admit he was right. "This is more like real life, I guess," I said. "Only without the boring parts."

"You mean real life on Earth is even more boring than this?" Minivan cried.

"Sometimes," I admitted. "For example, this is the second week of summer vacation and I'm bored out of my mind. That is, I was until I met you."

Minivan frowned. "Everyone on X-10 thinks Earth is like one long commercial," he said. "They're all dying to come here. My parents and I were very lucky to be chosen."

"Chosen for what?" I asked.

"To journey to Earth and bring back someone who can save our planet. Russell, please—you've got to help us!"

⇒ Chapter ⇐

4

At that moment, Minivan's parents walked into the room. "Ah, I didn't see you come in, Russell," his father said. He turned to his son. "I hope you two are becoming friends."

"Like a close friend of the family," his mother exclaimed, "the folks at the Sweet Dreams Funeral Home will help you plan the burial of your loved one."

"Mom, knock it off," Minivan said.

"Yes, you heard right!" his father said. "Big Bob's Auto World is prepared to knock ten percent off the price of every used car on the lot!"

"This is no time to be sociable!" Minivan shouted. "Russell knows we're aliens."

"Oh my!" his mother gasped. Then she and her husband began sneezing and burping to each other in Xarabibblian. Minivan joined in, and for the next few minutes it sounded like a bunch of Earth kids trying to gross each other out. Finally, Minivan's dad pointed his finger at the sixteen TVs. Zap! They all turned off, just like that.

"How do you do that?" I gasped.

"Oh, yeah, I promised to explain," Minivan replied. "After flashies got to be popular on our planet, many people had remote controls surgically implanted in their fingers." He held out his index finger. There was a tiny blue light glowing under the nail.

"We also have auxiliary audiovisual receiver antennas in our heads," his mother said proudly. "They improve reception, even in gale-force sandstorms."

That explained the weird bumps under their hair. "Minivan, you told me your family was chosen to come to Earth," I said. "If you're not planning to invade us, why are you here?"

"The people of Xarabibble-10 are not the invading type," Minivan's father said indignantly. "In fact, it's our planet that has been invaded."

"Russell, I know this must be a lot for you to absorb all at once," his mother said. "We didn't plan to reveal our identity to you this quickly. We wanted to learn our way around Earth a little better, maybe visit Disneyland and take the Universal Studios tour first. But since Minivan couldn't keep a secret, I suppose we'd better tell you everything."

Minivan rolled his eyes. "Mother," he groaned. "How much longer do you think we could have hidden the truth? We were just fooling ourselves, thinking we could pass as Earthlings. I mean, did you know that life on Earth is just a pale imitation of the flashies?"

"What?" his parents gasped. "No!"

"It's true," I said. "TV commercials—what you call flashies— are an exaggerated version of reality used to sell products to consumers."

Minivan's parents looked absolutely crestfallen. I thought

back to how I had felt when I first found out that Captain Spotless wasn't real. I must have looked pretty much the way the aliens did now.

"This is shocking news," Minivan's father said. "Still, it doesn't change the purpose of our mission." He turned to me. "Russell, X-10 has been taken over by barbarians from Praxbox-12. They've forced our people to be their slaves. Meanwhile, they spend all day watching flashies on our audiovisual receivers and eating our favorite snack foods."

His mother hung her head. "They don't let us watch," she said miserably. "And they won't even give us one lousy potato chip."

"Fortunately," Minivan continued, "a few brave Xarabib-blians have formed an underground movement to overthrow the invaders. We are part of that movement."

"Unfortunately," his father said, "our initial attempts to get rid of the Praxboxians were failures. We are a peaceful, entertainment-loving people. They are loud, smelly barbarians. To put it simply, they pounded us."

"Fortunately, our beloved chief came up with the idea of traveling to Earth for help," Minivan added.

"Unfortunately," his father said, "we don't have the technology to build a rocket ship that can travel from our galaxy to yours."

"Fortunately, our neighbors on Xarabibble-6 do," Minivan's mom said. "So they traded us a rocket ship for some sand."

"Sand?" I repeated uncertainly.

"That's right," Minivan replied. "X-10 has sand but no ocean. X-6 has ocean but no sand. In fact, their oceans are surrounded by barren fields of pointy rocks. Very bad for sunbathing."

His father nodded. "So, to make a long story short, we volunteered to come to Earth and get aid. Russell, will you help us?"

"Me? Gosh, Mr. . . . uh, Mr. . . ."

"Call me Motor Oil," Minivan's father said.

"And my name is Aspirin," his mother added.

I would have laughed if I hadn't been so stunned. "Motor Oil, Aspirin," I began, "I'd be happy to help you if I could. But I'm just a plain old Earth kid—and kind of an introverted one at that. I don't know the first thing about fighting alien barbarians."

"Oh, we don't expect *you* to fight the barbarians," Minivan said with a laugh.

"But who, then? I mean, sure, Earth probably has enough soldiers to fight the Para . . . the Paxa . . ."

"The Praxboxians," Aspirin said.

"Yeah, those guys. But we don't have spaceships that can travel all the way to Xarabibble-10. Besides, who knows if any Earth leaders would want to send their soldiers to—"

"Forget the soldier idea," Motor Oil broke in. "The Praxboxians have big guns and bad attitudes. They could wipe out your soldiers with one hairy paw behind their backs."

"Well, what about your neighbors on X-6?" I asked. "They sound like techno-wizards. Can't they come up with a way to disarm the barbarians?"

"Probably, but they're powerless to help us in any direct way," Aspirin explained. "You see, ever since we began trading sand with Xarabibble-6, it's become one of the most popular resort destinations in the universe. The Praxbox barbarians love X-6—or the Party Planet, as it's come to be called—and they spend millions of pan-galactic bartering units there every year. That's why X-6 signed a non-aggression pact with them just two months before they invaded our planet."

"Oh."

"But all is not lost," Minivan proclaimed. "There is still someone who can save our planet. And we have reason to believe you know how he can be contacted."

"Me?" I gasped. Last time I looked, I wasn't personally acquainted with any intergalactic bounty hunters or soldiers of fortune.

"Don't be modest," Aspirin said. "We know all about the wise teachings that you share with other people on the Internet. When it comes to flashies, no one on Planet Earth is more knowledgeable than you."

It was true Travis and I had started a bulletin board on the Internet devoted to TV commercials. But how would the aliens know that? "You have computers on your planet?" I asked in astonishment.

"No, but Xarabibble-6 does," Minivan explained. "They know all about that stuff."

My head was reeling. Aspirin was right. This was way too much information to absorb all at once.

"Please, Russell, don't toy with us," Motor Oil pleaded. "You must believe us when we tell you that only the most powerful creature in the universe stands a chance of saving our planet from the barbarian hordes."

"Only the strongest, the bravest . . ." Aspirin said.

"The smartest," Motor Oil added.

"The coolest!" Minivan cried.

"Who? Who?" I asked.

"Captain Spotless!" they all shouted.

31

"**B**ut Captain Spotless isn't real," I said. "He's just an animated character in a TV commercial—I mean, a flashie."

"What are you talking about?" Minivan asked. "He's big and tough, and he has superpowered soap bubbles that shoot out of his hands. I've seen it with my own two eyes."

"But he's only a cartoon," I insisted.

"What's a cartoon?" Aspirin asked.

"A two-dimensional drawing that—"

"Captain Spotless isn't a drawing," Motor Oil interrupted. "He moves."

"I know, I know," I said. "Animators make a whole bunch of drawings and put one on each frame of the video. Then when you watch the commercial, it looks as if Captain Spotless is moving."

"But he *is* moving," Minivan insisted. "He flies faster than germs can multiply."

"Yes," Motor Oil agreed. "Grit and grime are no match

for the Captain."

Then they all began to sing: "Captain Spotless came to call. Now we have no dirt at all. Thanks to the Captain, it's the truth—our whole house shines like his gold tooth!"

I let out an exasperated sigh. "Don't you aliens have any idea of how television works?"

"No," Minivan said.

"Well, it all starts with a television camera that records an image," I began. "The image forms in a tube that converts the light into an electric signal, splitting it into more than five hundred horizontal lines which . . ."

My voice trailed off. Motor Oil, Aspirin, and Minivan were gazing at me with vacant eyes and slack jaws. They looked as if they had suddenly fallen into a collective coma. "Are you all right?" I asked.

Minivan shook his head and his eyes began to focus. "I think I have a brain cramp," he said.

"The people on our planet aren't very good with numbers," Motor Oil explained.

"Or computers," Aspirin added.

"Or wires and plugs," Minivan said with distaste.

"Look, it doesn't matter," I said with a wave of my hand. "The only thing you need to know is that Captain Spotless doesn't exist. He's just pretend."

Suddenly, Aspirin burst into tears. "Why are you being so selfish?" she blubbered. "Can't you see we're desperate?"

"Please, Russell," Minivan pleaded. "Life on X-10 is totally bogus without flashies."

Motor Oil put his arm around his wife. "What is it you want?" he asked me. "We are a poor planet, but perhaps we can find some form of payment that will please you.

For example, do you need any sand?"

"I don't want your sand," I said incredulously. "I don't want anything from you."

Motor Oil lifted himself to his full height. Despite his pale moon face and his silly jogging suit, he looked pretty impressive. "We may not be technologically advanced, but we are not stupid," he said sternly.

"Well, not compared to the barbarians from Praxbox-12, anyway," Minivan added.

Motor Oil shot him a look, then turned back to me. "Clearly, you have some reason for not wanting to help us. What is it? We deserve to know."

I felt my knees quiver. The last thing I wanted was to get a bunch of outer space creatures mad at me. I mean, sure, they *said* they weren't going to vaporize me, but how did I know they weren't lying just to get on my good side?

"Look, I . . . I think you're talking to the wrong guy," I said with a nervous laugh. "I mean, haven't you seen any sci-fi movies? You're supposed to say, 'Take me to your leader.' "

They all stared at me blankly.

"Oh, uh, that's right," I stammered. "You only watch commercials. Well, hey, how about if I just give you directions to city hall and leave it at that?"

"If Captain Spotless doesn't wish to help us, that's up to him," Aspirin said seriously. "But at least let him tell us face-to-face."

"Yeah," Minivan urged. "Can't we just talk to him?"

I was so frustrated, I forgot all about being shy. "Don't you understand?" I practically shouted. "Captain Spotless is just a bunch of flickering dots on a TV screen. Asking him to save your planet is like asking a flashlight to recite Shakespeare!"

Aspirin burst out sobbing again. "Go home," Motor Oil told me, "and think about what you're doing. The fate of Xarabibble-10 is in your hands."

"It is not," I protested.

"Go! And if you choose wrong, may the sand of a thousand beaches clog your sinuses for all eternity!"

I know an insult when I hear one, even if it *is* a transgalactic insult. "Everyone on Earth thinks aliens must be super-intelligent," I said angrily. "Boy, would they laugh if they ever met you!"

The moment the words left my mouth, I wished I could take them back. After all, there was a time when I thought Captain Spotless was real, too, and I wouldn't want anyone calling *me* stupid.

But it was too late to turn back now. Motor Oil looked furious, and for all I knew he might suddenly decide to rearrange my molecules into something small and slimy. With my heart pounding, I climbed out the window and hurried home.

Back in my bedroom, I pulled off my jeans and crawled into bed. But I couldn't sleep. I kept thinking about Minivan and his family. They were so sincere and so desperate, I couldn't stay mad at them for long. In fact, the more I thought about it, the sorrier I felt for them. Their fellow Xarabibblians were counting on them, and now they were going to have to return home and tell the underground that their mission had been a failure.

But sympathy wasn't all I felt for Minivan and his parents. The more I thought about it, the more I began to feel . . . well, sort of strangely connected to them. Maybe it was because we both loved TV commercials so much. Or maybe it was because I knew what it was like to believe that the people you see in TV commercials are real.

I got up and walked down the hall to the bathroom. I splashed some cold water on my face and stared at myself in the mirror. It's a bizarre feeling to find yourself identifying with a bunch of aliens from outer space, and I guess I wanted to reassure myself that I was the same old Russell Brinkerhoff I had been before I met them. Luckily, I was—on the outside at least. I mean, I hadn't grown an auxiliary antenna on my head or anything. But inside . . . well, that was a different story.

I found myself wondering if maybe Minivan and his parents were right. Maybe Captain Spotless *was* real. Maybe the cartoon Captain Spotless I saw on the TV was just an artist's rendering of the real thing. Pretty soon my mind was racing, imagining that the makers of Spotless Cleanser had created the Captain in their laboratories by sprinkling a corpse with bathroom cleanser and then blasting it with electricity—sort of like a squeaky-clean version of Frankenstein's monster.

"Get a grip, Russell," I said to the boy in the mirror. "You've been watching too many horror movies."

Okay, so maybe I was getting a little carried away. Captain Spotless didn't live in a condo behind the Spotless Cleanser factory, and he wasn't going to fly to X-10 and fight off the barbarian hordes. But what if there was a way to make the Praxboxians *think* he was? Suppose, for example, the X-10 underground could create a life-sized hologram of the Captain and project him in front of the barbarians? Or what if they found a computer whiz who could create a virtual reality program where Captain Spotless destroys the Praxboxians?

I was so excited, I ran back to my room and turned on my computer. My plan was to log onto the Internet, track down a hologram specialist and a virtual reality programmer, and pick their brains. But before my modem could even begin dialing, I realized that my apparently premium plan was only store-brand quality.

Sure, a hologram of the Captain might frighten the barbarians for a few minutes, but if it couldn't talk or move it wasn't going to convince them to hop into their spaceships and blast off in search of bigger and better planets to enslave. Besides, once they found out they'd been duped, they'd probably exact a terrible revenge on the Xarabibblians—not to mention a certain Earth boy by the name of Russell T. Brinkerhoff.

As for the virtual reality scheme, that was even more lame. How were Minivan and his parents going to convince the barbarians to put on goggles and gloves and log onto computers? Even if they did, the creatures only had to hit the escape button to realize the stuff they were experiencing in the virtual world wasn't real. And then came the terrible revenge part, complete with the untimely death of little old me.

I pictured a pack of enormous, lice-infested barbarians squeezing my skinny body like a tube of Sparkle Toothpaste. With that image in my mind, I finally drifted off into an uneasy sleep.

⇒ Chapter ⇐

6

isten to this," my mother said at breakfast the next morning. "Two nights ago, a truck driver reported seeing a UFO land in the vacant lot at the end of our street."

I dropped my spoon in my Choco-Rock Cereal—the two-hundredth bowlful I'd eaten since Dad created their commercial and they had sent us a year's supply. "Let me see that."

My mom handed me the newspaper. Dad reached for his coffee cup and took a sip. "We're thinking of using a UFO in the new Bombs Away Burger ad I'm working on," he said. "You know, aliens come to Earth looking for the perfect burger, that kind of thing."

He began telling me the details, but I wasn't listening. I was too busy reading about the truck driver's description of a whirling globe of lights that had descended into the field at the end of La Cumbre Drive.

"It's true," I muttered with amazement. I guess deep down I was still wondering if I had hallucinated the aliens.

But here was proof—or at least a second opinion.

"What's true?" Mom asked, putting her coffee cup in the dishwasher.

I was dying to confess, but something told me Mom and Dad wouldn't believe me. "This guy really thinks he saw a UFO," I said.

She chuckled and shook her head. "People can convince themselves of anything. Well, I'm off. I'm doing a radio commercial for Busy Bee Markets at ten, then I'm recording a Zipsi-Cola jingle at two."

"Try to spend some time outside today, will you, Russell?" Dad said, grabbing his briefcase. "You're so pale."

"Maybe we should send *you* to survival camp," Mom suggested as she headed for the door.

"No!" I cried, jumping to my feet. "I'll go outside. I might even walk down to the park and rent some Rollerblades."

Mom looked at me doubtfully. I had never strapped on a pair of Rollerblades in my life. "So long, Russell. I'll be back by four."

"Have a good day, son," Dad said, following her out the door.

After they left, I flopped down on the couch and hit the remote. My favorite Zipsi Cola ad was on, but I couldn't concentrate. I kept thinking about Minivan and his family and wondering what they were doing. For all I knew, they might have already left for X-10. The thought gave me a hollow, achy feeling inside. I'd barely known the aliens for forty-eight hours, but already I'd grown attached to them.

I got up and looked out the window at Minivan's house. I was dying to know what was going on in there. Finally, I couldn't stand it any longer. I had to find out if they were still around. I thought about walking over and ringing the doorbell, but after the argument we'd had last night I wasn't sure they'd be pleased to see me. So I decided to sneak into the bushes and spy on them again.

I wasn't in the mood to have another close encounter with that thorn bush, so this time I crawled into the flowering bushes at the side of the house. I lifted my head until my forehead cleared the windowsill and found myself peering into the aliens' living room. My heart leaped. Minivan and his parents were there, standing side by side in the middle of the room. The two dozen TVs were on.

I looked closer. The aliens were gazing down at something on the floor and yammering away in Xarabibblian. It appeared to be a gray box about the size of a suitcase. Lying on top of it was a computer floppy disk.

Motor Oil picked up a spiral binder from the top of one of the TVs and opened it. Then he knelt down and held up a wire that was attached to the side of the box. Minivan and Aspirin pointed and chattered. Motor Oil looked from the book to the box to the floppy disk. Finally, he dropped the wire and gave the box a kick.

Nothing happened. The aliens threw up their hands and groaned.

I shook my head. Motor Oil wasn't kidding when he said Xarabibblians weren't good with wires and plugs. I mean, these guys were absolute techno-morons. And then I realized something. This was my chance to start over with the aliens. Maybe I couldn't give them Captain Spotless, but there was a chance I could make their little gray box do whatever it was meant to do.

With my heart in my throat, I tapped on the window. The

aliens turned and saw me. For a moment nobody moved, and I began to wonder if they were about to zap me to a cinder. Then Minivan's wide face broke into a grin.

"Russell," he cried, rushing over and throwing open the window, "awesome news! Dad called X-6 and they sent us instructions on how to contact Captain Spotless!"

"But how?" I asked with astonishment.

"We're going to zap him out of the television set . . . or something like that," Minivan said. "Dad wrote down the instructions."

"You see, we don't need your help," Motor Oil said in a proud voice. "We're going to ask the Captain ourselves."

"Spoken like a typical X-10 man," Aspirin said, walking over to the window. "The truth is, Russell, Motor Oil has spent the last two hours trying to make sense of the instructions, and all he's got to show for it are paper cuts and a pounding headache."

"Just give me a few more minutes," Motor Oil insisted. "I've almost got it figured out."

I was dying to see what was written down in that notebook. And what were the floppy disk and the gray box supposed to do? Could Motor Oil actually bring Captain Spotless to life? My brain told me it was impossible, but every fiber of my being was wishing and hoping it was true.

"I could . . ." I began hesitantly, ". . . that is, I wouldn't mind . . . I mean, would you like me to, you know, help?"

"But I thought you said you didn't know how to contact Captain Spotless," Motor Oil said suspiciously.

"I don't," I said, "but I'm pretty good at figuring out instructions. In fact, I'm the only one in my family who can program our VCR. Besides," I added, "I want to meet

41

Captain Spotless as much as you do."

"But you told us he wasn't real," Minivan pointed out.

"He was lying," Motor Oil cried. "I knew it!"

"I was telling the truth," I said, "at least, what I *thought* was the truth. But if the scientists of X-6 know a way to bring the Captain out of the TV, I want to help. That is . . . if you'll let me."

"When help is needed, the friendly folks at Tiny Tom's Tow Service are there to lend a hand!" Aspirin said with a smile.

"Hand in hand, heart to heart," Minivan added, reaching out to pull me through the open window. "At Little Apple Preschool, we care about your kids!"

Aspirin began to sing, and we all joined in: "Benchmark Greeting Cards are there, to say the things that you can't say. Reaching out to those you love, let's make today a special day."

Everyone smiled, including Motor Oil, and I knew we were friends again. Eagerly I walked over to the gray box and picked up the notebook.

"Wow, your handwriting is hard to read," I said.

"Oops, that's Xarabibblian," Motor Oil replied. "Let me translate."

As Motor Oil translated, I wrote out the instructions in English. "Okay, so according to this," I said, skimming the sentences, "the floppy disk is a super-sophisticated 3-D drafting program and the gray box is a quantum particle pattern-recognition device."

"It is?" Aspirin said. "Gosh, we used it as a step stool on the spaceship."

"What we do is scan an image of Captain Spotless and enter it into a computer using the 3-D drafting program.

Then we link the computer to the quantum-particle device and the television, and wait until a Captain Spotless commercial comes on. With the help of the computer program, the box will track the pattern of the Captain on the screen, lock onto it, and shoot a beam of focused electro-magnetic energy at it. Then . . ."

My voice trailed off as I double-checked the instructions. I could barely believe what I was reading. "Then if all goes well," I continued in a hushed voice, "the atom particles that make up Captain Spotless will be sucked out of the TV tube and reconstituted right here in your living room."

"Pure and fresh," Minivan said enthusiastically. "Golden Grove one hundred percent reconstituted orange juice is jam-packed with vitamin C."

He smiled expectantly, waiting for my response. But I was too stunned to be quoting TV commercials now. If the instructions from X-6 really worked, we would be creating life right before our eyes. The concept was absolutely mind-boggling.

"This is incredible!" I said. "Do you realize what would happen if the people of Earth knew this box existed? They'd probably start World War Three trying to get their hands on it."

"Earth people start wars?" Aspirin asked with dismay. "But they seem so friendly and peaceful in the flashies."

"This planet is really starting to bring me down," Motor Oil said. "All I want to do is get back home and stretch out in front of my A-V receiver with a six-pack of Zipsi-Cola and big bag of fried pork rinds."

"That's my dream, too," Aspirin said wistfully. "But it will never happen as long as the Praxboxians control X-10."

43

"Please, Russell," Minivan pleaded, "hurry! Make Captain Spotless appear."

"Hang on," I said. "According to the instructions, we're going to need a scanner and a computer that can run this 3-D drafting program. We're talking at least 1.5 gigabytes of memory—much more than my little PC can handle."

Minivan's eyes were starting to glaze over. "My brain hurts," he moaned.

"Relax. I'll take care of the programming," I said. "We just need to buy a few things. Uh, do you folks have any money?"

Motor Oil checked his pockets. "I have sixteen pan-galactic bartering units."

I sighed. Somehow I was going to have to come up with some serious bucks, and fast. Then I remembered my father telling my mother about a new credit card he had gotten just for emergencies. He had put it in the top drawer of his desk in the den and said to my mom, "It's here just in case something big comes up."

If this isn't something big, I thought, *I don't know what is.*

But would Dad understand? I tried to picture what I would say when he got the bill. "You see, Dad, it turns out the next-door neighbors are aliens and, well, we needed to buy a state-of-the-art computer to get Captain Spotless out of the TV and—"

Okay, so maybe I wouldn't put it in those words exactly. I decided I'd figure it out later, after Xaribbible-10 was saved and I was a transgalactic hero.

"I'm going to the mall," I said. "Stay here, and I'll be back in an hour."

"Take me!" Minivan cried. "I'm dying to see what Earth is really like!"

"Oh, yes," Motor Oil agreed. "We can't return to X-10 without a glimpse of Earth life."

"But what if someone starts a war?" Aspirin asked anxiously.

I laughed. The odds of war breaking out at the Valley Mall were pretty slim—unless, of course, someone noticed the aliens' auxiliary antennas or the blue lights under their fingernails and figured out they weren't from this solar system.

The thought made my stomach roll like the sun-dappled seas in the Sunlight Tuna commercials. But at the same time, I was excited. How often does an Earth kid get to give a family of outer space creatures a tour of his hometown? It was too outrageous.

And yet what if we were found out? Minivan and his family didn't exactly blend in. I pictured police officers and FBI agents surrounding us, me being dragged off for questioning, the aliens being carted away to who-knows-where. Meanwhile, everyone on X-10 would be waiting for Captain Spotless to show up and save the planet. Only he'd never come—and it would be all my fault.

And then I remembered my father's new credit card. No credit card, no computer. No computer, no Captain Spotless. But what were the odds the sales clerks at Circuit Central were going to let an eleven-year-old buy an expensive computer with a credit card? Zilch. On the other hand, they'd have no trouble selling it to grown-ups—say, Motor Oil and Aspirin.

Suddenly, the choice was simple. "Come on, you guys," I said. "Let's go to the mall."

⇒ Chapter ⇐

7

"**W**hat happened to the colors?" Minivan asked, peering uncertainly up and down La Cumbre Drive. "Everything's all washed out."

"The sun went behind a cloud," I said. "It's just overcast, that's all."

We were standing at the end of the street, waiting for the bus. My father's credit card was in my pocket, pressing uncomfortably against my leg and reminding me that I was about to do something highly illegal. But glancing at the aliens, I realized credit card fraud was the least of my worries.

Out in natural light Minivan and his parents looked even more peculiar than they had inside their house. Their faces were as round and wide as pie pans, their skin seemed more blue than white, and their oversized sneakers looked like clown shoes. Plus, considering it was a warm summer day, the hats and gloves they were wearing to hide the antennas on their heads and the blue lights under their fingernails looked totally bizarre.

A rusty old car with a crushed fender drove by, spewing carbon monoxide. "What's wrong with that car?" Aspirin coughed.

"It's old and the exhaust system is shot," I explained.

"In the flashies, all the cars are new and clean," Minivan said.

Aspirin tugged on the too-small Dodgers cap I had given her to wear. "I thought people who owned cars were happy and carefree and attractive," she said. "That man looked old and grumpy."

"I love old Earthlings!" Motor Oil exclaimed. "They're spry and feisty, and they use laxatives."

"Can we buy some laxatives today, Russell?" Minivan asked. "I've always wanted to try them."

I winced. "Hey, you guys, there are some things you just don't talk about in public."

The aliens weren't listening. They were singing: "Peace of mind is just a spoonful away—"

"Stop!" I cried. "You can't go around singing every time the mood strikes you."

"Why not?" Motor Oil asked. "They do in the flashies."

"But real life is not the—"

"Oh, look," Minivan cried, "the bus is coming!"

The bus pulled up to the curb and the door opened. "Public transportation," Motor Oil proclaimed. "The fast, clean way to say yes to Mother Earth!"

"That's what they tell me," the driver said in a bored voice, staring out the front window. Then he turned and saw the aliens. His eyes grew wide. "Fifty cents each," he said. "And move to the rear."

"Can I put the money in the box, Russell?" Minivan

47

asked eagerly. "Please? Please?"

The bus driver looked at me. "These folks with you?"

I could feel myself blushing. I wanted to say no. I wanted to run away, back to my cool, dark house.

"Russell is our friend," Minivan said loudly. "He's taking us to the mall."

I glanced up at the bus windows. Everyone was staring at us.

"Fifty cents each," the driver repeated. "And make sure you keep an eye on them."

"Yes, sir," I muttered, dropping the change in the box.

"*I* wanted to do that," Minivan protested.

I grabbed his arm and dragged him to the back of the bus. Motor Oil and Aspirin followed. "Look, there's Chauncy!" Aspirin exclaimed, pointing to a Prime Cut Dog Food ad on the wall. "But why isn't he moving?"

"Sit down!" I hissed. They did—in the middle of the bus. "On the seats!" I cried. They sat, but their rear ends barely touched the plastic.

"Why is everyone so mean?" Aspirin asked. "Why aren't they singing and offering us breath mints?"

"Because they think you're inmates from an insane asylum," I whispered. "You have to be quiet and keep your eyes down. This is a city bus, not a TV commercial."

"I don't like it here," Minivan whined, scratching his head beneath his red wool ski cap. "I want to go home and watch our A-V receivers."

"TVs," I said. "They're called TVs here. And you were the one who wanted to come, so just be quiet, okay?"

The aliens hung their heads and fell silent. I leaned back in my seat and breathed a sigh of relief. At the same time, I felt a little sorry for them. After a diet of TV commercials, real life was bound to be a letdown.

"Valley Mall," the driver called, turning into the parking lot.

"Come on," I said, "we're here."

I hustled the aliens off the bus, ignoring the curious stares of the other passengers. Then I led them into the mall.

Almost immediately the aliens perked up. "Ooh, this is nice!" Aspirin exclaimed. "The colors are bright, just like on our A-V—I mean, the TV."

"That's because of the fluorescent lights," I said. "It's not natural."

"Who cares?" Motor Oil replied. "It's pretty. And look at those flowers. The leaves are so green—just like in the flashies."

"They're fake," I told him.

"Wow! Look at all this stuff!" Minivan cried, stopping in front of a drug store. He ran inside and headed down the aisles, picking up bottles and boxes at random. Motor Oil, Aspirin, and I ran after him.

"Sparkle Toothpaste and Dentu-Brite Dental Floss!" he exclaimed, stuffing them into his pockets.

"Cherish Hair Coloring and Doodah Candy Bars!" Aspirin squealed ecstatically.

"Rich milk chocolate, creamy caramel, and crunchy peanuts in every bite," Motor Oil said in a deep announcer's voice. "Take a Doodah break today." He ripped open a candy bar and chomped down on it. Then he spit it out on the floor.

"Ew!" I cried. "Why did you do that?"

"I keep forgetting we can't eat Earth food," Motor Oil

said. "It's bad for us and it tastes horrible. On X-10 we eat food that looks like your snack food but contains all the nutrients we need. The X-6 scientists make it for us."

"Look!" Minivan cried, careening down the toy aisle. "World of War Action Figures!" He threw back his head and bellowed at the top of his lungs: "Woooorld of Waaaar Action Fig-ures! *Pow! Pow! Blam! Blam! Boom!*" He grabbed one of the tanks and ripped off the plastic.

"Hey, stop that!" I cried.

A man wearing an assistant manager's badge appeared at the end of the aisle. "Can I help you?" he asked.

Minivan was down on his knees, moving the tank along the floor the way the kid does in the commercial. "You can drive a tank," he sang, "or toss a grenade, capture bad guys, and save the day."

The assistant manager looked at Motor Oil and Aspirin. "I hope you're planning to buy that."

"Buy now, pay later at Crazy Carl's Midnight Madness Sale!" Motor Oil shouted, pulling off his blue beret and tossing it into the air.

The man reached inside his jacket and pulled out a walkie-talkie. "Security to aisle six," he said into the mouthpiece.

But Minivan and his parents were already heading toward the exit. As they ran back into the mall, I managed to pull the toothpaste and dental floss out of Minivan's pockets and toss it back inside the store.

"Circuit Central is this way!" I shouted after them.

But the aliens had other plans. They burst into a clothing store where Aspirin immediately grabbed an armful of dresses off the rack and spun around like a fashion model.

I ran in just as a perky salesclerk approached. "What size are you looking for, ma'am?" she asked.

"You're a cook, a housekeeper, a mother, and a busy executive," Aspirin said. "Yes, you're the modern woman, and we've got your wardrobe. Max Reed Coordinates . . . because you deserve it all."

"Uh, yes," the clerk said, her smile fading. "Well, I'll just let you browse a bit."

"Do you have Cheetah Basketball Shoes?" Minivan asked.

Motor Oil grabbed a pair of sunglasses from a nearby counter and put them on. "Run fast, jump high," he said in the super-cool voice of the Cheetah athletic shoes mascot, Chill Cheetah. "And don't forget to stuff it!"

The clerk's mouth fell open. "I beg your pardon!" she gasped.

I felt like I was in a horrible nightmare, the kind where you're walking through the mall and everybody's staring at you, and then you suddenly realize you've forgotten to wear clothes. Only hanging out with the aliens was even more humiliating than going out in public naked.

"It's time to go, you guys," I said, waving my hands in front of their faces. "Now!"

"Time is running out on our 'Buy One, Get One Free' weekend!" Minivan exclaimed. "So bring your buns down to Goldberg's Bakery and take home a few of ours."

This was getting serious. The aliens had slipped into some sort of weird consumer frenzy. Their eyes were shiny, their hands were trembling, and their voices were about an octave higher than normal. I tried to catch Minivan's eye but he stared past me as if he didn't even see me.

I looked toward the door. By now, mall security was probably on our tails. I pictured them dragging us into a back room, searching us, and finding my dad's credit card in my pocket. The thought gave me the courage to speak up, instead of crawling into a dressing room and cowering under the bench.

"Attention shoppers!" I shouted. "For a limited time only, Chill Cheetah is here at the Valley Mall giving away free basketball shoes. That's right, I said *free!*"

"Chill Cheetah!" Minivan squealed.

"Free basketball shoes!" Motor Oil exclaimed.

"Where? Where?" Aspirin cried, dropping the dresses.

"Proceed immediately to Circuit Central!" I yelled. "Repeat, Chill Cheetah is in Circuit Central!"

The last word had barely passed my lips when the aliens sprinted out of the clothing store, knocking over a couple of mannequins on the way, and took off across the mall.

≫ Chapter ≪
8

"**I** liked the mall," Minivan said. "It was fun!"

"It had all the things we see on the flashies, only we could reach out and touch them," Motor Oil sighed. "It was a dream come true."

We were back in the aliens' living room. Motor Oil, Minivan, and Aspirin were watching commercials on TV and chatting happily about their trip to consumer heaven. I was supposed to be setting up the computer and the scanner, but I was having trouble concentrating. The events of the morning kept replaying in my mind. I pictured the aliens running wildly through the drug store, pulling dresses off the racks at the clothing store, and bursting into Circuit Central, demanding to see Chill Cheetah.

And then there was the horrible moment when Motor Oil used my father's credit card to buy the computer and the scanner, and signed his name in Xarabibblian. Naturally, his signature looked nothing like the signature on the back of the card. Good thing I managed to convince the salesclerk that my so-called father had recently been struck by lightning, causing massive changes to his nervous system. Considering how strange Motor Oil looked, I guess it wasn't tough for the clerk to believe *something* was wrong with him.

"I just wish we could have met Chill Cheetah," Aspirin said, channel surfing with her index finger.

"I guess we just missed him," I lied. There was no point bothering to explain that Chill Cheetah didn't exist, and even if he did he wouldn't be in Circuit Central giving away basketball shoes.

"Can we go to another mall tomorrow?" Motor Oil asked eagerly.

"Tomorrow you're going to be whizzing through space, on your way back to X-10 with Captain Spotless," I said. "Providing I can get this drafting program working, that is."

Minivan turned from the wall of TVs. "We're going to miss you, Russell."

"I'm going to miss you, too," I answered, and I meant it. I never would have thought I could feel close to a bunch of space aliens, but I did. Meeting them was kind of like going back in time and meeting myself at age five—only with pale blue skin and ape feet. And they were the only intelligent life forms I'd ever met, including Travis, who loved TV commercials as much as I did.

On the other hand, hanging around with Minivan and his family was a little like bobsledding through an avalanche blindfolded. I never knew what bizarre, out-of-control, and possibly humiliating thing was going to happen next. As soon as they left, I planned to lock myself in my house, plant myself in front of the TV set, and not move until school started.

"Okay," I said, hitting the ENTER key on the computer, "the drafting program is up and running. Now let me see those instructions again."

"Russell, how tall is Captain Spotless?" Motor Oil asked as I began entering facts and figures into the computer.

"Oh, I don't know. Considering how he looks in the commercials, I'd say maybe eight feet."

Motor Oil swallowed hard. "The Praxboxians are ten feet tall, and really strong. Is the Captain strong?"

I still couldn't believe we were talking about a cartoon character as if he was a real person. Of course, assuming the X-6 scientists knew what they were talking about, he *was* real—or soon would be, anyway. "You've seen him in the commercials," I said. "He can clean an entire house with one blast of his superpowered soap bubbles."

"Yes, but the barbarians aren't just dirty," Motor Oil said. "They're smelly and selfish and low-down mean. And they can devour a jumbo bag of potato chips in a single bite."

"But Motor Oil," Aspirin broke in, "the chief said Captain Spotless would save our planet. How can you question our brave and brilliant leader?"

"I'm not," he said quickly. "But if one superhero is good, then wouldn't two be even better?"

"What are you getting at?" I asked.

"Well, Chill Cheetah is really strong and powerful, right?" Motor Oil said. "Why don't we take *him* back to X-10, too?"

I paused, my fingers poised over the keyboard. I could barely get my brain around the idea of bringing Captain Spotless to life; I certainly hadn't considered using the box to zap any other commercial characters. But now that Motor

Oil mentioned it, why not? I mean, this was my chance to meet all my old childhood heroes in the flesh. I'd be crazy to pass it up.

"You don't want Chill Cheetah," I said. "He's strong and fast, and he can slam-dunk a basketball like Michael Jordan, but he has a habit of turning soft around little children."

"That's true," Minivan agreed. "Remember that flashie where he goes one-on-one with a little boy and finally lifts him up to score the winning basket?"

Aspirin nodded. "Praxboxian children aren't exactly small and lovable, but we'd better not take any chances."

"You're the TV expert, Russell," Motor Oil said, bending his body into one of his weird sitting-in-midair positions. "Who would you pick to fight the barbarians?"

I didn't have to stop and think. After all, I'd been fantasizing about this kind of thing since I was a little kid. "I'd choose Lady Bug from the BugBeGone insect spray commercials," I said.

"Of course!" Minivan exclaimed. "She uses her beauty to lure unsuspecting insects to her side, then she hits the spray nozzle on the top of her head and blasts them with poison."

I nodded, picturing her beautiful human face, flowing red hair, four arms, insect shell, and antenna. "If she can rub out a kitchen full of nasty roaches, I figure she'll have no trouble with a few barbarians."

"Okay," Motor Oil said, "who else?"

Everyone began talking at once. Soon the aliens and I were lost in a noisy debate about which commercial characters would be able to crush the barbarian invasion. For a while we considered Rad Rabbit, star of the Radoline Motor

Oil ads. He was fast and clever, but probably too small to do much damage. Then there was the Sunlight Tuna. He was a good swimmer, but we all agreed that wouldn't be much use on a planet without an ocean.

Finally, we decided to go with my old favorite, Chauncy, the big brown-and-black dog from the Prime Cut Dog Food ads. He wore a studded silver collar and walked on his hind legs like a person. I didn't know how tough he was, but there was no doubt he was smart—just check out the commercial where he's dressed like Sherlock Holmes and uncovers the dog food that his rival, Princess Poodle, hides under the sofa cushions.

Our last choice was the Stickky Elves—Bo, Bill, Bert, and Binky—stars of the Stickky Adhesive Tape commercials. They were small, speedy, hard-working elves who wore green Robin Hood-style clothes and carried rolls of adhesive tape on their belts. We figured we could use them to run under the barbarians' feet and distract them while the other commercial heroes pounded them. They could also use their tape to tie up fallen bad guys.

"Okay," I said, "so it's decided. We're taking Captain Spotless, Lady Bug, Chauncy, and the Stickky Elves."

"Yes!" the aliens shouted in unison.

"Now we have to scan their images and enter them into the computer," I explained. I could have waited for the commercials to appear on TV, taken a photo of the TV screen, and then scanned the photos. But I had a better idea. "Wait here," I said. "I'll be right back."

I ran home. My father has been collecting animation cels—the individual cartoon images that animators draw to create animated films and videos—since before I was born.

Naturally, he especially loved to collect cels from TV commercials.

I went into his den and looked around. Among the dozens of framed cels that lined the walls were cels of Captain Spotless holding a garbage can, Lady Bug spraying a frightened roach, Chauncy eating a dish of Prime Cut, and the Stickky Elves wrapping a birthday present. I carefully removed them from the wall and hurried back to the aliens' house.

Minivan and his parents were waiting at the front door. They watched impatiently while I ran the cels through the scanner and entered the necessary data. "There," I said at last, "that should do it."

I hit a key and the characters appeared on the screen, looking exactly as they did on TV—except, of course, they weren't animated. I tapped a few more keys and we were able to view them from different angles—top, bottom, right profile, left profile.

"Make them come out," Minivan demanded, banging on the computer screen with his knuckles.

"They aren't going to come out of *there*," I explained as I connected a wire between the computer and the quantum-particle pattern-recognition box. "They'll come out of the TV—*if* this box really works, that is."

"Oh, do it, Russell!" Aspirin cried, hopping from foot to foot like an impatient toddler. "Hurry!"

"I will, but we have to wait for the characters to show up on the TV so the box can track their images and blast them with electro-magnetic energy."

"I don't get it," Motor Oil said blankly.

"Just sit down and watch the flashies," I replied. "If you

see a commercial for Spotless Cleanser, BugBeGone Bug Spray, Prime Cut Dog Food, or Stickky Adhesive Tape, let me know."

The aliens sat in front of their television sets for exactly thirty seconds. "I can't wait!" Minivan cried, leaping up. "I'm going to explode!"

"We want Captain Spotless!" Aspirin moaned, bursting into tears.

"Make him come to life, Russell," Motor Oil wailed. "Now!"

Soon all three of them were crying and banging their fists on the floor. "Now! Now! Now!" they whined.

My head was pounding. I felt like a teacher in a preschool full of oversized brats. I put my hands over my ears and tried to think. Then suddenly it hit me.

"I've got an idea," I said loudly. "We've got four VCRs at my house—one for each of our TV sets—plus lots of commercials on videotape. I'll get the VCRs and the videos of the commercials we need and bring them back here. Then we'll play them all at once and see if we can zap the Captain, Lady Bug, Chauncy, and the elves out of the TV at the same time."

Instantly the aliens stopped crying and began jumping up and down. "Oh boy! Oh boy!" they shouted. "We're going to meet the Captain!"

I had to smile. The aliens looked totally blissed out. I just hoped they weren't building themselves up for a big letdown. I mean, was this box really going to work? I just couldn't believe it. Still, the aliens' enthusiasm was catching. With my heart in my throat, I ran to my house again and lugged back the videos and the four VCRs.

Quickly, I set up the VCRs, popped in the tapes, and cued them up to the correct commercials. Then I connected the pattern-recognition box to the VCRs with an extension cable I'd found in my father's toolbox. Finally, I positioned the aliens in front of the VCRs. "When I say go, I want you to push the PLAY buttons," I told them.

I sat crosslegged in front of the computer screen. With trembling fingers, I tapped the keys to call up the 3-D images of the Captain, Lady Bug, Chauncy, and the elves. I took a deep breath. It was now or never. "Go!" I cried.

The aliens hit the PLAY buttons and the four commercials flashed simultaneously onto four TV screens. "Okay, here goes nothing," I said under my breath as I leaned forward and flipped the ENGAGE switch on the pattern-recognition box.

The box began to hum. I held my breath. Suddenly there was a flash of blinding light and an ear-piercing blast of white noise. I closed my eyes, covered my ears, and fell back onto the rug. Then the room fell silent and I heard the aliens gasp.

I opened my eyes and crawled to my knees. What I saw was almost too much for my tiny Earth brain to comprehend. Captain Spotless, Lady Bug, Chauncy, and four tiny Stickky Elves were standing in front of the televisions. They weren't two-dimensional cartoons, and they weren't 3-D computer simulations either. They were *real*.

Chapter 9

For one long moment, nobody moved. Captain Spotless, Lady Bug, Chauncy, and the Stickky Elves stared at us, and we stared back at them.

Then complete chaos broke loose.

"Where in blue blazes am I?" the Captain bellowed, tossing aside the garbage can. He turned and glared down at me. He was at least twice my height and a good three hundred pounds of solid muscle. I wasn't sure which gleamed brighter—his pure white uniform and cape or his gold tooth.

"Well, uh . . . uh . . ." I stammered. "It's kind of a long story. You see—"

"Captain Spotless!" Aspirin squealed like a teenage girl swooning over her favorite rock star. "Oh, it's really you! I just can't believe it!"

"What happened?" Lady Bug demanded in a shrill voice. "My dress is all wrinkled, and my hair is a mess!" Two of her hands reached down to smooth her tight black dress while the other two fluffed up her cherry-red hair. She snapped her gum. "Well, don't just stand there," she said to no one in particular. "Bring me a mirror, and make it snappy."

Funny, I thought, *I never noticed Lady Bug chewing gum in the BugBeGone commercials.*

Motor Oil didn't seem to notice. "She's beautiful," he sighed. "Oh, Lady Bug, I—"

"I say, old chap, where are your manners?" Chauncy broke in. He had a snooty English accent, and when he talked, he sprayed saliva in all directions. "You don't invite guests into your home without offering them refreshments. Make mine a pound of Prime Cut Dog Food in a silver bowl, if you please."

I was so surprised, I couldn't think of anything to say. I wasn't sure which was stranger—hearing a dog talk, or finding out that Chauncy wasn't the lovable, tail-wagging pooch I'd thought he was. I glanced over at the aliens. Motor Oil and Aspirin looked kind of stunned, but Minivan was too fixated on Captain Spotless to pay attention to Chauncy.

"Wait till the Praxboxians see you!" he exclaimed, reaching up to squeeze the Captain's bulging bicep.

"Get your filthy hand off me!" Captain Spotless ordered in the voice of a Marine drill sergeant. "When was the last time you took a bath?"

"I . . . I . . ."

The Captain grabbed Minivan and bent his pale, rounded ears back. "Look at this! You could grow potatoes in the dirt back here!" He shook his fist and a mass of superpowered soap bubbles appeared at his fingertips. Then he began to violently scrub Minivan's ears.

"Don't!" Minivan whimpered. "Ow! Ow!"

"Eeeeek!"

Everybody turned toward Aspirin, who was pointing at the rows of TVs with a look of horror on her face. We followed her finger and saw that the Stickky Elves were standing on the top of the multi-level shelving unit, sticking adhesive tape all over one of the TV sets. In the blink of an eye—just like in the commercials—they had completely wrapped up the TV. The only problem was they weren't using wrapping paper. Just tape.

"Oh, our beautiful A-V receiver!" Aspirin moaned.

"What are you doing?" Motor Oil cried. "Stop! Stop!"

But the elves just giggled and set to work. Faster than you could say "product endorsement," two of them lifted the TV up over their heads while the other two scrambled to the top of the set and taped it to the ceiling.

Wow, I thought, *I had no idea the Stickky Elves were so strong.*

Rrrrip!

I stopped thinking about the elves and started thinking about the tape. It was beginning to peel from the ceiling. The TV slipped lower and lower.

"No!" Minivan wailed, rushing to the shelving unit and starting to climb.

But it was too late. The TV fell from the ceiling and hit the floor with a sickening crunch.

"Oops!" the elves said in unison. They blushed and giggled with embarrassment.

Then Bo, the chubbiest elf and the biggest—he must have been all of twelve inches high—grinned and said, "Let's try again!"

The elves giggled in their tiny munchkin voices and headed for the next TV, singing merrily as they went: "Stickky Tape, it's really strong. Stickky Tape, it lasts so long."

"Stop!" Minivan shouted, jumping up and swiping at the elves.

They just snickered and pulled out their tape dispensers. In the blink of an eye, they wound Stickky Tape around Minivan's hand and stuck it to the TV.

"Hey, let me go!" he cried. He struggled and strained, but he couldn't pull his hand away. The elves jumped up and down and shrieked with laughter.

"How childish," Chauncy said in a bored voice. He turned to me. "Can't you see I'm absolutely famished? Bring on the Prime Cut or I'll make doo-doo on the carpet!"

"We don't have to *see* you," Captain Spotless growled. "We can smell you. What did you do—roll on a dead skunk?"

The Captain was right. Chauncy *was* pretty ripe.

"I beg your pardon, you muscle-bound blimp," Chauncy said coolly. "Have we been formally introduced?"

"How would you like a flea bath?" the Captain asked, walking menacingly toward him.

"Don't come any closer," Chauncy warned. "I bite, and I haven't had my rabies shot."

Lady Bug stepped between them. "Have you checked out the kitchen?" she asked the Captain. "The cabinet under the sink is crawling with mildew."

"What?" he bellowed. "This is a job for Captain Spotless!" He leaped into the air and flew into the kitchen, knocking the door off its hinges in the process.

Lady Bug turned to Chauncy. "What a handsome puppy you are," she said in a sugary voice. "How'd you like me to scratch your tummy?"

Chauncy's growl turned to a grin. "I never say no to an offer like that," he replied, falling on his back with his legs in the air.

Lady Bug began to stroke Chauncy's tummy. Instantly, a dozen fleas sprang out of his fur. She glanced down at them and her sweet smile turned cold and calculating. Slowly, quietly, she reached up to the spray nozzle on the top of her head and pressed it down. A blast of toxic spray enveloped Chauncy from nose to tail.

"Aah-oooh!" he howled, leaping to his feet. He tore across the room, nearly missing Motor Oil and Aspirin, who were trying to unravel the tape from Minivan's hand. While they worked, the Stickky Elves were scampering between their legs, handcuffing their ankles with adhesive tape.

"Wait!" I yelled. "Don't—"

But before I could get another word out, Chauncy doubled back across the room and plowed into Minivan.

"Whoa!" Minivan cried. He lost his balance and careened backward, pulling the TV off the shelf. As he fell, he knocked into Motor Oil and Aspirin. All three of them tumbled to the floor. The TV set fell too, missing Chauncy and one of the elves by mere inches.

"This is a job for Captain Spotless!" the Captain boomed, zooming back into the living room. His pure white cape smacked Lady Bug and me in the face as he flew past. We both jumped backward, fell into each other, and landed on the floor.

At that moment, the Captain let loose a blast of

superpowered bubbles. Within seconds we were shoulder-deep in soapsuds.

Everyone began screaming at once.

"What's the big idea, you iron-pumping moron?" Lady Bug shrieked. She tried to stand up, but the soapsuds were so slippery she only managed to flap her arms a few times and fall backward onto her shell.

"I have never been so humiliated in my life!" Chauncy cried, shaking soap bubbles in all directions.

"Help!" the elves squealed. "We're drowning! We're drowning!"

Minivan struggled to his knees and managed to catch my eye. "Russell," he shouted above the din, "do something! Please!"

Me? Why me? It hadn't been *my* idea to release Captain Spotless and his cohorts from the television set. I had been perfectly happy watching them in their nice, friendly commercials and imagining they were kind, helpful creatures who wanted to save the world from dirt and disorder. Instead, they were turning out to be snippy, self-centered lunatics.

But there was no time to point that out now. If someone didn't do something fast, there was a good chance we were all going to die of suffocation by soap bubbles.

Without thinking, I struggled to my feet, jumped onto one of the smashed and slimy TVs, and screamed at the top of my lungs, *"Will everyone please shut up!"*

≫ Chapter ≪

10

*A*mazingly, it worked. Everyone stopped screaming and struggling and turned to me with expectant looks on their faces. Apparently they thought I was going to take charge. Too bad my mind had gone completely blank.

"Uh . . . uh," I stammered, blurting out the first words that popped into my head, "my name is Russell and, uh, if you want to know what's going on, you'd better do what I say."

Nobody put up an argument, so I kept talking.

"Captain Spotless, stop blasting us with soap bubbles," I said in what I hoped was a take-charge kind of voice. "Motor Oil, find the Stickky Elves. Aspirin, take the tape off Minivan's hand. Chauncy, flip Lady Bug over and help her up. Then I want all of you to follow me."

I marched into the kitchen, hoping no one would notice that my knees were knocking together. A few moments later they all joined me, looking wet and bedraggled and angry.

"What's going on?" Captain Spotless demanded. "One

minute I'm disinfecting a toilet bowl and minding my own business. The next minute I black out, and when I wake up I'm here in this stinking joint."

"Yes, what *is* this place?" Chauncy asked, looking around. "It seems decidedly second-rate to me."

"This is the real world," I told them. "You know, the place where the people live who buy the products you advertise."

"The real world?" Lady Bug repeated, wrinkling her nose. "Never heard of it."

"Why are the colors so drab?" asked Binky, the smallest Stickky Elf. "Everything looks washed out."

"That's what *we* wanted to know," Minivan said excitedly. "It turns out this is what Earth looks like. It's not nearly as nice as the flashies—I mean, TV commercials. I mean, *your* world."

"That's why we need you to help us," Motor Oil added. "We must defeat the Praxboxian invaders and make Xarabibble-10 safe for couch potatoes once more."

"Safe as a babe in his mother's arms," Aspirin proclaimed. "That's the peace of mind you get with Bondo False Teeth Bonding Solution."

"No more false starts," Motor Oil chimed in. "With Radoline Motor Oil, your car will start first time—every time—in rain, sleet, and snow."

The aliens grinned at each other and burst into song: "Snow-Ball Cupcakes, yum, yum, yum! They taste so good in your tum, tum, tum!"

"Come on, join in!" Minivan urged.

Captain Spotless, Lady Bug, Chauncy, and the elves just stared at him.

"What in tarnation are you creatures jabbering about?" Captain Spotless demanded.

Chauncy put his paws over his ears. "Stop that hideous caterwauling! Stop, I say!"

The aliens' voices trailed off into silence. They looked like a group of overeager Christmas carolers who had just been pelted with tomatoes.

"Uh, maybe I'd better take over," I said with a nervous laugh. I turned to Captain Spotless and his cohorts. "You see, it's like this . . ."

As clearly and simply as I could manage, I explained to the TV characters what was going on. I told them about X-10 and the flashies and the barbarians. I explained about the quantum-particle pattern-recognition device which had snatched them from the television set and brought them here. Finally, I explained about the important mission that awaited them on Xarabibble-10.

"Let me get this straight," Chauncy said, gazing at me skeptically. "You want *me* to go with these people in jogging suits and help them fight a race of big, hairy animals."

"Well . . . er . . . yes, that's pretty much sums it up."

"Let's leave right now," Minivan said eagerly. "Dad, get the spaceship ready."

"Good idea, son." Motor Oil headed for the back door, but Captain Spotless reached out and grabbed him by the collar.

"Hold it right there, bub," he said. "I don't know about the dog, the bug lady, and the short people, but I'm not going anywhere except back where I came from."

"That's right," Lady Bug said, fluffing up her flowing hair. "I'm not going to waste my sizable talent on a bunch of barbarians—whatever *they* are. I've got bigger fleas to fry."

"But you *have* to help us," Minivan cried, turning to the Captain. "You're Captain Spotless, the most powerful creature in the entire universe!"

"And you're a pale blue kid with dirty ears," he shot back. "So what?"

Minivan's face fell. I knew how he felt, because I felt the same way. Nothing was turning out the way we'd planned it. All this time we'd been expecting the TV characters to be brave, selfless superheroes who would jump at the chance to save a planet full of flashies fanatics. Instead, they were small-minded superpains who just wanted to get back to what they were doing before they were so rudely interrupted.

That's when it hit me. Maybe the reason the superheroes had no interest in making the world safe for TV commercials was because they had no idea what a TV commercial—or even a TV—was. Maybe as far as they were concerned, the stuff they did in TV commercials was real life. In fact, maybe it was their entire world.

I decided to test my theory. "I know you all want to get on with your lives," I said to the TV characters. "And you'll be able to do that very soon." It was a total lie, of course. I had no idea how to get them back into the TV, but they didn't have to know that—at least, not now.

"Well, that's the first good news I've heard since I hit this junk heap," the Captain growled.

"But Russell," Minivan said anxiously, "we can't—"

"You must miss your world very much," I continued, ignoring him.

"Of course we do," said Bill, an elf with big ears and a goatee. There were tears in his eyes.

"Tell us about it," I said. "I mean, what does your world look like? Where do you live? What do you do all day?"

70

"I clean stuff," Captain Spotless said.

"I kill bugs," Lady Bug said.

"I find dog food and eat it," Chauncy said.

"We put tape on things," the elves said in unison.

"Sure," I replied, "we know that. But what do you do when you aren't working?"

"What's working?" Chauncy asked.

"Well . . . let me put it this way," I said. "When you aren't cleaning and killing and eating and taping, what do you do?"

They all thought about it for a moment, their brows furrowing with concentration. Suddenly, Captain Spotless's face brightened.

"I clean stuff," he said.

"I kill bugs," Lady Bug said.

"I find dog food and eat it," Chauncy said.

"We put tape on things," the elves chimed in.

Wow, talk about boring! Maybe the world of commercials wasn't as exciting as I had imagined. Still, I was happy because it meant my theory was correct. And that gave me an idea on how to convince Captain Spotless and the gang to do what we wanted.

I turned to the Captain. "You think Minivan is dirty?" I said. "You should see his planet. The place is a pigsty."

The Captain's eyes brightened. "Really?"

I nodded. "Dirt, mildew, germs everywhere. And the bugs—yuck! The planet is overrun with them."

"No fooling?" Lady Bug asked with interest. She pulled out a compact from the pocket of her dress and began powdering her nose.

The aliens finally caught on. "And then there are those

71

barbarians we told you about," Motor Oil said. "Not only have they taken over our TVs, they've also hidden all our dog food."

Chauncy pricked up his ears. "You eat dog food?" he asked.

Aspirin nodded. "Prime Cut is our favorite."

Chauncy's tail flew back and forth. "Let me at it!" he panted.

"On X-10," Minivan said, "no one would dream of visiting a friend without taking a can of Prime Cut along—gift-wrapped, of course."

"Ooh, you must use a lot of tape!" exclaimed Bert, a freckled elf in wire-rimmed glasses.

"They do," I agreed.

"I want to go to Xarabibble-10!" the little elf cried, jumping up and down. "Take me, take me!"

"Me, too!" the other elves joined in.

"Don't forget me, big boy," Lady Bug cooed.

"All for one and one for all," Chauncy said.

"Take me, or I'll wash out your mouths with Spotless Cleanser," the Captain ordered.

I grinned. "Get the spaceship ready, Motor Oil."

But instead of looking happy, Motor Oil was frowning. "Can I talk to you a second, Russell?" he whispered. "Outside."

I walked out the side door and joined Motor Oil in the driveway. "What are we going to do when we get to X-10 and the flashies characters find out we don't eat dog food and wrap packages all day?" he asked.

"Oh, you'll think of something," I replied. "I mean, you said the barbarians are dirty, right? That should be enough for Captain Spotless. And if they have fleas, then Lady Bug—"

"It sounds so simple when you explain it," Motor Oil broke in. "But let's face it, we aren't experts like you. We don't know how to talk to them the way you do."

"Me?" I had to laugh. "I have no idea what I'm doing. I just wait until I'm in a total panic and then say whatever pops into my head."

"Don't be modest," Motor Oil said. "You have Captain Spotless and the others in the palm of your hand. That's why you have to come back to Xarabibble-10 with us and lead them into battle against the barbarian hordes."

"What?" I gasped.

"It won't take long. We'll just zip to X-10, crush the barbarian invasion, and bring you right back. You'll be home in time for dinner."

"And what am I supposed to tell my parents?" I asked. "'Mom, Dad, the next-door neighbors are going to outer space this afternoon and they asked me to come along. Please, may I?'"

"Russell," he said seriously, "I pride myself on having a good working knowledge of technical matters—for a native of X-10, that is. For example, I'm the only one on the planet who can adjust the color control on our A-V receiver."

"That's nice, but—"

"This is very embarrassing for me to admit, Russell, but I've forgotten how to fly the spaceship." He shrugged. "The scientists from X-6 showed me, but I guess I kind of spaced out."

"But you managed to fly from X-10 to Earth," I pointed out.

"Sure, because it was preprogrammed on X-6," he said. "But it's up to me to program it for our return to X-10. Russell, please," he begged, grabbing my hand. "Without your help, we'll probably crash and burn before we even reach Jupiter."

"But . . ."

"Russell, I'm not asking for selfish reasons," he pleaded. "Aspirin, Minivan, and I are just unimportant, expendable Xarabibblians. But Captain Spotless, Lady Bug, Chauncy, and the Stickky Elves are superstars. You just can't send them off to die in the vacuum of space."

"Well, when you put it that way . . ."

"Oh, Russell," Motor Oil cried, "say yes and you will go down in the history of Xarabibble-10 as our beloved hero and savior!"

How could I not be flattered by a promise like that? Besides, I had to admit it would be pretty exciting to travel through outer space, visit another galaxy, and save an entire planet—providing I lived to tell about it, that is.

I swallowed hard. "Need a loan? Call the dedicated professionals at Cashco Financial Services. We love to say yes."

Motor Oil let out a whoop of joy and began dancing up and down the driveway, singing, "If you need a loan, and you want the best . . ."

Trying to ignore the knot in the pit of my stomach, I joined in: "Call the guys at Cashco, we love to say yes!"

⇒ Chapter ⇐

11

Motor Oil burst into the kitchen. "Russell is coming to X-10 with us!" he announced.

"Yippee!" Minivan cried.

Aspirin was so excited, she threw her arms around me and started babbling in Xarabibblian. I hugged back and tried to ignore the fact that she was sneezing into my neck.

When Aspirin finally calmed down, I glanced over at the TV heroes. They couldn't have cared less about Motor Oil's good news. In fact, they had already gone back to the only activities they knew how to do. Captain Spotless was cleaning out the refrigerator. Lady Bug was on her hands and knees, luring ants from under the sink. Chauncy was sniffing around for Prime Cut, and the elves were taping the kitchen chairs to the wall.

While they worked, I got busy figuring out a way to convince my parents to let me leave the solar system. "Aspirin, I want you to call my house at exactly six o'clock and pretend to be my best friend's mother," I said. "Her name is Muriel Turner. Tell my mom you're going to visit Travis at survival camp in Oregon and you want to invite me to come along. Say you're leaving tonight at eight, you're going to camp out in your motor home along the way, and you'll be back next week."

"Oh, boy!" Aspirin said eagerly. "Just like in the flashie where the mother phones her son's friends and invites them to a surprise party at Magic Land Amusement Park."

"Well, sort of," I replied. "Only don't act so perky or my mom will know you're not Mrs. Turner. Try to sound kind of harried and worn out . . . like this." I pretended to be Travis's mother. "Hello, Jane. This is Muriel Turner." I put my hand over an imaginary phone receiver and shouted, "Be quiet in there, you kids! Can't you see I'm talking on the phone! Turn down that TV or you're going to get a time-out!"

"Gee," Minivan said, "the mothers in the flashies never sound like that."

"That's because they don't have six kids, including two sets of twins," I explained. "Okay, Aspirin, think you can handle it?"

"When there are grease stains on your apron, let Shake-N-Scrub handle it," she sang. "When the baby spills the grape juice, let Shake-N-Scrub handle it!"

Please, I prayed, *just don't let her burst into song while she's talking to my mother.* "I'll see you in a couple of hours," I said, heading for the door.

"Wait, don't leave us!" Motor Oil cried, grabbing my sleeve. He motioned toward Captain Spotless and the gang. "What if they try to run away or something?"

"Bring in some dirt and ants from the yard for the Captain and Lady Bug," I suggested. "Tell Chauncy that Princess

Poodle hid his Prime Cut in the basement. As for the elves, just tell them you need to wrap some TVs to give as presents, then stand back."

"Russell, you're brilliant," Aspirin said admiringly.

I tried to imagine what my parents would say if they knew I was planning to blast off into outer space with three aliens and a bunch of TV commercial mascots. Somehow I doubted that *brilliant* would be the first word that came into their minds.

I pushed the thought out of my head. "Don't forget to call my house at six o'clock," I said. "And Aspirin, please try to sound exhausted."

"Oh, boy, this is going to be fun!" she exclaimed, sounding about as exhausted as a rabbit on caffeine.

"I sure hope so," I said, forcing a smile. Then I headed for home.

For dinner that evening Mom made Sunlight Tuna Surprise, which was actually not very surprising since she had cooked it at least once a week for the last two months. We were sitting in the kitchen with the TV on, waiting for Dad's newest Zipsi-Cola commercial to premiere on the network news.

"Here it comes!" Dad exclaimed, pointing to the TV.

I watched the computer-animated cola cans dance the cha-cha, and wondered what they'd be like if they were hooked up to the aliens' pattern-recognition box and zapped out of the TV. I had always thought the cans seemed so energetic and athletic; in fact, I used to fantasize about playing on a baseball team with them. But after meeting Captain Spotless and the gang I wasn't sure *what* to think.

"Dad, don't you think the Zipsi-Cola cans seem a little hyper?" I asked.

"What? You think the animation is choppy?" he asked with concern.

"No, I mean their personalities. What do you think they're like in real life?"

Dad looked at me quizzically. "Real life? Russell, they're computer-animated soft drink cans."

"I *told* you he needed some new friends," Mom said. "He spends all day watching TV."

"So do I," Dad pointed out.

"But you're an advertising executive. Russell is still an impressionable child. Who knows what all that TV viewing is doing to his mind?"

"Maybe you're right," Dad said with a nod. "I'm going to ask the Turners for the address of that survival camp."

"But Mom, Dad—" I began.

Just then, the telephone rang. Mom picked it up. "Oh, Muriel," she said, "we were just talking about you. How's everything?"

I held my breath.

Mom smiled uncertainly. "I'm glad to hear that," she said. She paused. "Really? Really? You don't say. Let me run it past my husband."

"What is it?" Dad asked.

"The Turners are driving out to visit Travis at camp and they asked if Russell wanted to go along," Mom said. "They're leaving tonight and they'll be back next week. It's kind of short notice, but I think it might be good for him."

"It's perfect," Dad replied. "This is just what Russell needs to get him away from the TV for a few days." He turned to me. "What do you think, son?"

"Sounds like fun!" I said with a big grin.

Mom talked a few more minutes, then hung up. "I've never heard Muriel Turner sound so happy," she said, sitting down at the table. "She was practically giddy. When I asked her how she was, she started singing the Big Mouth Bubblegum theme song."

"She hired a new baby-sitter," I said. "I think it's really cheering her up."

"Oh. Plus, when I asked her if she was planning to stay in motels, she said they were going to cramp up along the way."

"Camp out," I said a little too quickly. "I mean . . . er, that's probably what she meant, don't you think?"

"Yes, I suppose so. Tom and Muriel Turner have always been a little scatterbrained." She chuckled and patted my hand. "Better get packed, Russell. The Turners will be here to pick you up in two hours."

I ran to my room and started packing—not for a camping trip to Oregon, but for a journey into outer space!

Two hours later, I heard a horn honk outside our house. I ran to the window and peeked through the miniblinds. The aliens' moving van was idling in the street.

"It's the Turners," I said, grabbing my bags. I ran to the sofa where Mom and Dad were watching TV and gave them each a quick kiss. "See you next week."

"Wait a minute, Russell," Mom said, getting to her feet. "I want to talk to Tom and Muriel before you take off."

But I was already out the door and sprinting across the lawn to the truck. Motor Oil was sitting in the driver's seat with Aspirin and Minivan beside him. There was no sign of the TV creatures. "Hurry up!" I called. "My mother's coming!"

Minivan threw open the door and I squeezed in beside him. "Let's go!" I urged.

Motor Oil struggled to put the truck into gear. I saw my mother standing at the front door, squinting uncertainly into the darkness. Fortunately the street was dark and she wasn't wearing her glasses.

"Is that a new motor home?" she called, stepping off the porch. "It looks much bigger than the one I remember."

"Big Eddie's RV Paradise made our dreams come true!" Aspirin proclaimed.

"Big Eddie's got sixty acres of rip-roaring recreational vehicles," Minivan drawled. "Y'all come on down and check 'em out, ya hear?"

I elbowed him in the ribs and called, "Gotta hurry, Mom. If we don't get to the RV park in Santa Cruz by midnight, we'll lose our space."

Motor Oil finally jammed the truck into gear and hit the gas. With the tires squealing, we jerked down the street and careened around a curve.

"Where did you learn to drive?" I shouted.

"I didn't," Motor Oil replied. "But I've seen plenty of driving in the flashies. My favorite is the E-Z Lube Motor Oil commercial with Lamar Stanwell."

"But Lamar Stanwell is a professional race car driver!" I cried. "Regular people don't drive the way he does."

"They don't?" Motor Oil asked, bouncing over the curb and roaring into the vacant lot at the end of the street. He pulled the key out of the ignition. The engine gasped and died. We rolled another fifty feet, hit a eucalyptus tree, and stopped.

"Now what?" I asked, wiping beads of sweat from my forehead.

Before anyone could answer, we heard a loud rattling from somewhere behind us. I jumped out of the front seat just in time to see Captain Spotless, Lady Bug, Chauncy, and the Stickky Elves throw open the doors at the back of the truck and pile out.

"What's the big idea?" Captain Spotless demanded. "Why did you lock us in that rat hole?"

"We were bouncing around like pinballs!" Bo, the chubby elf, squealed. "We had to tape ourselves to the floor."

"Ooh, bugs!" Lady Bug suddenly exclaimed, falling on her knees and eyeing a potato bug that was crawling through the dirt. "Come to mama, you handsome thing."

"Don't wander off," I warned. "We're just about to blast into space—I hope." I turned to the aliens. "What do we do first?"

Motor Oil climbed into the back of the truck and pushed a button on the wall. "Stand back," he warned, jumping out.

As I stood watching, my mouth agape, the truck's wheels disappeared into the body of the trailer and were replaced by hydraulic legs. The legs pushed the truck up onto one end so that the cab was pointing toward the sky. Aerodynamic wings and a tail sprouted out of the top and sides. Finally, a door popped open in what had once been the bottom of the truck, and a set of steps automatically unfolded.

"Awesome!" I breathed.

"Yeah, not bad," Minivan said. "But the really cool part is

that it's got a working A-V receiver on board. We watched flashies the entire way here!"

"Now, if you can just figure out the controls, we're in business," Aspirin added.

I climbed on board and looked around. There wasn't much to see—just a computer console, an A-V receiver, a bathroom, a refrigerator, and one small window.

I walked up to the computer and flipped the ON switch. Luckily, the flight software wasn't much more complicated than the NASA Flight Simulator computer game Travis got for Christmas last year. Plus, there was an instruction booklet under the keyboard. It was in Xarabibblian, of course, but Motor Oil translated it for me. Within minutes, we were ready to go.

"Come on, everybody," I called, walking out of the ship. "Let's get out of here before someone sees us."

Captain Spotless and his cohorts were wandering through the vacant lot, cleaning, spraying, searching, and taping amidst the scrub brush and eucalyptus trees. We rounded them up and hustled them into the spaceship. Then the aliens stood in front of the computer console and motioned for me to join them. Restraining harnesses dropped from a panel in the ceiling and we buckled ourselves in.

I looked over my shoulder at the TV characters, wondering if they needed to buckle up, too. They were pacing around the ship, searching for something to clean, spray, eat, or tape. It was pretty unlikely they'd stand still long enough to be strapped in, I decided. Besides, Captain Spotless was too big and the elves were way too small.

I opened the computer instruction booklet and punched

in the coordinates for Xarabibble-10. Then I called up the file entitled "Take-off Procedures" and typed in the commands. It was so simple—more like a computer game than real life. I hit the ENTER key automatically, barely pausing to think about what I'd done.

Instantly the ship began to vibrate and hum. I felt my heart kick into overdrive. This was no computer game! This was an honest-to-gosh UFO, and it was about to take off into outer space!

I looked over at the aliens. They had turned on the A-V receiver with their remote-control fingers and were happily singing along with a Bombs Away Burger commercial.

Suddenly I felt a wave of panic surge through me. I was trapped in a spaceship, about to blast off into the unknown with seven cartoon characters and three aliens who had the combined IQ of a pebble.

"Wait!" I cried, fumbling frantically with my harness. "I can't leave the solar system now! I have a book due at the library and there's a *Bewitched* rerun I absolutely *cannot* miss!"

At that moment there was a deafening *whoosh* and I felt the spaceship begin to move. I lurched out of my harness and staggered to the window. The ship was zooming through the sky, heading for the stars. Below us lay Planet Earth, getting smaller by the second.

Chapter

12

I leaned against the window, eyes shut tight, gasping for breath and quivering like a plate of Jell-O. "I'm flying through outer space," I whispered over and over again in a shaky voice. "I'm flying through outer space."

I kept expecting something horrible to happen. Maybe my face would be pulled apart like a hunk of Silly Putty from the intense G forces. Or maybe the spaceship would blow up or be hit by a meteor or something. But none of that happened. Gradually, almost in spite of myself, I started to calm down.

I opened my eyes and looked out the window again. The sky was ablaze with stars. Then suddenly a comet with a long, vaporous tail whizzed past the window, so close I was sure I could touch it.

"Wow! Did you see that?" I exclaimed, but no one was looking. Motor Oil, Aspirin, and Minivan were stretched out as if they were in easy chairs—except without the chairs, of course—watching flashies on the A-V receiver. At the moment they were completely engrossed in a baby food commercial.

"Minivan, check this out," I called. "We're passing Mars. Look, you can see craters and mountains and everything!"

But Minivan wasn't listening. He and his parents were singing along with an Australian soft drink commercial. Aspirin noticed me looking at them and motioned me over. "Come on, Russell," she urged, "join in!"

I shook my head and looked around for the TV guys. The Stickky Elves were hanging from the ceiling by long pieces of tape, swinging back and forth and giggling like mice on laughing gas. I took one look at them and sighed. Trying to discuss the beauty of outer space with them would be like trying to explain quantum physics to a drooling six-month-old.

I noticed Lady Bug going through the refrigerator, tossing cans of soda and cartons of imitation cheese spread over her shoulders with her four hands as she searched for bugs. I was about to invite her to join me at the window when I remembered something my health teacher once told the class. It seems all human beings have tons of microscopic insects called mites hopping around in our eyelashes. I quickly decided the less time I spent talking face-to-face with Lady Bug, the better.

Suddenly I noticed something out of the corner of my eye. I spun around to find Chauncy ripping my backpack open with his teeth. Within seconds he had found the sample cans of Prime Cut Dog Food I had taken from our pantry and packed for him. He sniffed them, his tail wagging frantically, and began trying to gnaw them open with his teeth.

I turned away. There was no point trying to talk to Chauncy when he was focused on Prime Cut. That left Captain Spotless. Somehow I had a hunch he would share my excitement at seeing the solar system close-up. After all, he was a bonafide superhero. In my mind, I had always thought of him as the Superman of TV commercials. I pictured him flying among the stars, keeping the universe safe from grit and grime.

I found the Captain crouching in the bathroom, attacking the grunge around the bottom of the sink. "Hi," I said, leaning against the door. "There's a really awesome view of the sky out the window of the ship."

He turned and stared down at me as if I was a particularly nasty patch of mildew. "So?"

"So . . . er . . . I was just wondering," I stammered. "We're about to pass Jupiter. Do you want to watch it with me?"

The Captain glared at me. "Is that dirt I see under your fingernails?" he growled, shaking his fist threateningly.

I shuddered, remembering the scrubbing he'd given Minivan's ears. "Quick, look behind you!" I cried. "What's that stuff growing in the toilet?"

The Captain spun around and sent a blast of soap bubbles flying toward the toilet. I slammed the door and hurried back to the window. So much for getting up close and personal with Captain Spotless.

The universe zipped by, mile after endless mile of planets, stars, comets, and meteors. But now, with no one to share it with, it didn't seem so beautiful. Instead, I was overwhelmed by the vast emptiness stretching out before me. I thought about my parents far, far away on Planet Earth, and I felt a sudden wave of loneliness wash over me.

The drone of the A-V receiver pulled me out of my daydream. I turned and watched the aliens happily shouting out the words to a Whisper Soft Toilet Tissue ad. Without even realizing what I was doing, I inched a little closer.

Next, a Sunlight Tuna commercial came on. I had seen it dozens of times before and I knew every camera angle by heart. Soon I found myself mouthing the familiar words along with the announcer. When the theme song began to play, the aliens sang along.

"From the sun-dappled seas where dolphins roam," they crooned, "we bring our tuna to your home."

I joined in on the last two lines. "Sunlight tunas are happy fish. A tasty treat in any dish."

Minivan grinned at me and I smiled back. I was starting to feel a little better. I scooted over and sat beside him. After a few seconds of static, a Prime Cut Dog Food ad flashed on the screen. Chauncy appeared, chasing Princess Poodle through a garden.

"Look, Chauncy," Minivan exclaimed, "it's you!"

Chauncy looked up from the can he was gnawing. In the commercial, Princess Poodle had just hidden a bowl of Prime Cut in a rabbit hole.

"Aah-ooooh!" Chauncy howled, just like in the commercial. Then he took off running at full speed across the spaceship and flung himself against the screen of the A-V receiver.

Crash! The screen shattered into a million pieces. Chauncy let out a yelp and fell back to the floor, along with a few wires from the inside of the receiver that were caught around his paws.

"Oh, no!" Motor Oil wailed. "Our A-V receiver is ruined!"

"Good gracious, forget the silly box!" Chauncy cried. "Can't you see I've been injured?"

I ran over and checked him out, but except for one small cut on his nose he seemed fine. "Do you want me to get some Prime Cut for you?" I asked.

"Oh, no," he said sarcastically, "it's so much more fun to suck on the can and dream."

I took a can opener out of my backpack. The second I popped it into a can, Chauncy began jumping up and down and drooling. "Hurry up!" he complained, nipping at my legs. "Can't you see I'm practically fainting from hunger?"

I set the can down and Chauncy leaped on it. Then I turned back to the A-V receiver, only to discover that the Stickky Elves were crawling all over it, trying to tape the glass back into place. The only problem was that they hadn't fit the pieces together first, so the screen looked like a jigsaw puzzle that had been put together by a lunatic. Plus, the wires were still dangling out of the hole where the screen had once been. Binky, the smallest elf, was taping them to the volume control.

"Russell, *do* something," Minivan begged.

"Yes, Russell," Motor Oil whined, "make the elves stop."

"Then fix our receiver," Aspirin pleaded. "Please!"

"I can't," I said. "Even if the elves can tape the screen back together, the image will be practically unwatchable. And the sound—" I ripped off the tape and turned up the volume, but there was only silence. I shrugged. "I'm afraid it's broken."

Instantly the aliens threw themselves to the floor and burst into pitiful sobs. "What are we going to do?" Aspirin sniffed.

"We won't be back on Xarabibble-10 for another two hours," Motor Oil moaned.

"I want my flashies!" Minivan wailed. "I want my flashies!"

I rolled my eyes. I knew if I had to listen to the aliens cry and complain for another two hours, I'd go out of my mind. I had to do something. But what?

Then suddenly I had an idea. I ran to my backpack and returned with a pencil and paper. "Have you guys ever played tic-tac-toe?" I asked.

"What's that?" Minivan asked between sobs.

"It's a game. I think you'll like it." I drew four lines on the paper and put an X in the middle.

"What's a game?" Motor Oil asked.

I stared at him. "You know, *games*. Hide-and-seek, Kick the Can, stuff like that. Then there are board games like Monopoly and Scrabble. And sports like basketball, baseball—"

"Chill Cheetah plays basketball in the flashies," Aspirin said with a nod. "He pushes an orange ball through a metal hoop lined with string."

"Well, yes, that's part of it," I replied. "But there's a lot more to basketball than that. There are two teams, and they play on a court with wooden floors. And there are rules and strategy, and—"

"I'm confused," Minivan whimpered.

"Wait a minute," I said. "Are you telling me you don't have games on X-10?"

He shook his head.

"I can't believe it. What do you do all day?"

"We told you," Motor Oil said. "We watch flashies."

"But before the flashies," I insisted. "What about then?"

"We searched for sand fleas to eat," he replied.

I tried not to gag. "You eat sand fleas?"

"Sure," Aspirin replied. "All the snack food you've seen us eating is just processed sand fleas. They're hard to catch, too."

"I'll bet."

"When we weren't out hunting fleas," Motor Oil continued, "we mostly sat in our huts, watching the wind blow the sand around. But that was in the dark days, before X-6 contacted us and we began trading sand for A-V receivers."

I sat there for a moment, trying to take it all in. I felt kind of sorry for the people of X-10. Imagine living in a world with no games, no sports, no stories, no music, no nothing. It was easy to understand why the planet was so obsessed with TV commercials. Compared to hunting for sand fleas, watching flashies was the thrill of a lifetime.

"Let me show you how to play tic-tac-toe," I said. I explained the rules and demonstrated a few possible moves.

Minivan scratched his head. "It looks hard."

"Give it a try," I said encouragingly. "I bet you can do it."

With Motor Oil and Aspirin looking on, Minivan and I began to play. When it was Minivan's turn, he spent so much time considering his moves you'd have thought we were playing championship chess. But eventually, after three or four games, he began to get the idea. He was still losing, but at least he understood the rules.

"Can I ask you a question?" I said, drawing an X in the corner square to begin our tenth game.

"The friendly folks at Seven Day Tire Stores are always eager to answer your questions," Motor Oil replied.

I smiled. "Are the real-life TV characters the way you thought they'd be? I mean, take Captain Spotless, for example. Before you met him in person, how did you picture him?"

"Brave and strong," Minivan said. "And, well . . . not such a bully." He touched his ears and winced.

"They're all different from the way I imagined them," I

said with a nod. "Chauncy is so snooty and sarcastic. Lady Bug is awfully vain, and the elves are always making trouble." I shrugged. "I don't know. They just seemed a lot more fun when I used to watch them on TV."

"The flashies are the best," Motor Oil said emphatically. "Better than X-10, better than Earth, better than *anything*."

Minivan drew an O in one of the squares. "Uh . . . tic-tac-toe?" he asked uncertainly.

I looked down at the paper. I couldn't believe my eyes. "You did it!" I exclaimed. "You won!"

Minivan let out a whoop of joy. "I won! I actually won!"

I held out my hands, palms up, and Minivan slapped them. Then all four of us jumped out of our seats and hugged each other. We were so happy that anyone would have thought Minivan had just won an Olympic medal. Even the TV creatures stopped cleaning and spraying and eating and taping to stare at us. But we didn't care. We were having fun.

Suddenly, the computer began to beep loudly. I untangled myself from the aliens and hurried over. According to the information on the screen, we were beginning our descent toward Xarabibble-10. "We're about to land," I announced.

Motor Oil, Aspirin, and Minivan began jumping up and down and squealing with delight. Captain Spotless stamped his feet, Lady Bug took out her makeup, Chauncy barked, and the elves giggled.

"Home sweet home!" Motor Oil cried. "Let the caring agents at Coast to Coast Realtors make your dream come true."

"Buy Farmer's Pride Sausage," Aspirin shouted, "for that authentic down-home taste!"

The aliens' enthusiasm was contagious. With my heart pounding, I ran to the window and looked out. Xarabibble-10 lay below us, an enormous brown planet covered with huge, swirling yellow blobs.

I've never felt such a rush of emotion in my life. I was ecstatic, awed, and scared to death all at the same time. Here I was in a distant galaxy, light-years from Earth, about to land on alien soil. In fact, within minutes I would become the first human being in the history of mankind ever to set foot on a planet other than Earth.

I was still trying to get my head around that concept when an ear-splitting whine sent me reeling backward, my arms wrapped around my head. Then the spaceship began to spin and shake. All of us—humans, aliens, and cartoon characters alike—were tossed together like pieces of gravel in a cement mixer.

I was beginning to wonder if any of us would survive the landing when suddenly there was a roar, a jarring thump . . . and silence. Slowly I untangled myself from Lady Bug's four arms, pulled my foot out from under Captain Spotless's rear end, and stood up.

Then the door of the spaceship opened and a deep, disembodied voice emitted a burst of burps and sneezes, followed by the words "Welcome to Xarabibble-10!"

Chapter

13

While I stood there with my heart in my throat, Minivan walked over and looked out the door of the ship. I'm not sure what I expected him to find on the other side— maybe a welcoming party of joyous Xarabibblians ready to lift us onto their shoulders, or possibly a horde of barbarians eager to chomp our heads like so many sticks of Big Mouth Bubblegum. But to my surprise, there was no one there. In fact, there was nothing at all outside the ship except a high, curved stone wall.

"Where's all the sand you told me about?" I asked, stepping up behind Minivan.

"It's out there," he said. "You just can't see it right now because we're on a secret underground landing pad."

"But where are the Xarabibblians?" I asked.

"Back in their huts," he explained. "When the barbarians invaded, they made us their slaves. We spend our days serving them snack food and brushing the sand fleas out of their hair."

"But what about that voice?" I asked. "Someone said,

'Welcome to Xarabibble-10.' "

"That was a tape recording of our brave and brilliant chief, the Honorable Dental Floss," Minivan said.

"Dental Floss?" I tried not to laugh.

Minivan wasn't even smiling. "Yes. He recorded it at great personal risk to himself in order to welcome you and Captain Spotless to our planet. The barbarians are holding our beloved chief under house arrest. He is forbidden to watch the flashies and must eat nothing but spiny chucka."

"What's that?" I asked.

"A foul-tasting plant covered with thorns. We only eat it when we can't find enough sand fleas. It's the pits."

"What in blue blazes are we waiting for?" the Captain roared, elbowing his way to the door. "Lead me to the dirt!"

"Did I hear someone say 'sand fleas'?" Lady Bug purred, tapping me on the shoulder with her four index fingers.

"I'm famished!" Chauncy panted, scratching at my leg. "Where's that Prime Cut you promised?"

"Yes, and the packages that need to be wrapped," said the chubby elf named Bo. The rest of the elves jumped up and down and giggled in anticipation.

Motor Oil grabbed my sleeve and pulled me aside. Aspirin and Minivan crowded around him. "We can't let them out of the ship," Motor Oil whispered anxiously. "Not until we meet with the underground."

"When will that happen?" I asked.

"Tonight, after the barbarians doze off in front of the A-Vs, we'll all meet here and you will be introduced to our beloved chief. Until then, we have to return to our hut and go about our daily chores as if nothing unusual has happened."

"But how can you do that? You've been missing for days.

How will you explain to the barbarians where you've been?"

"We already took care of that," Aspirin said. "When the X-6 scientists gave us this spaceship, they told the Praxboxians they were taking us back to X-6 with them to help unload a new shipment of sand. When we got to X-6, they programmed the ship for us and we took off for Earth."

Minivan nodded. "When we get home, we'll tell the barbarians we were delayed by bad weather on X-6."

"Cut the small talk!" Captain Spotless shouted, pushing himself among Motor Oil, Aspirin, and me. "I'm ready to do some scrubbing!"

".Just a few more minutes," I lied. "We're waiting for a police escort that will drive you to the dirtiest spot on the planet."

The Captain let out a roar of delight and shot soap bubbles into the air. I turned to the aliens and whispered, "Go back to your hut. I'll do my best to keep the TV guys busy here."

"No, no," Aspirin protested. "You have to come with us."

"What?" I gasped. "Why?"

"If you don't get a look at the Praxboxians, you won't know what is needed to defeat them," Motor Oil said.

Minivan nodded. "It's like tic-tac-toe, Russell. You have to plan your moves."

I gazed at Minivan, impressed. He was really starting to use his brain. Unfortunately, this was one time I would have preferred him to remain stupid. I had absolutely no desire to meet a bunch of hairy, smelly barbarians up close, especially if I was going to be expected to act as their personal hairdresser.

"I can't go with you," I argued. "Once the barbarians see I'm an Earthling, they'll know you weren't on X-6 unloading sand. And then, who knows what they might do." I pictured myself stuffed and mounted on the wall of their hut like a big game trophy.

"They won't recognize you," Aspirin said. "Not after you put on the disguise the X-6 scientists created for you." She walked to the computer console and knelt down to take something out of a cabinet underneath. "A little makeup, new clothes, a few accessories, and no one will know the difference."

"We hope," Motor Oil added cheerfully.

I swallowed hard. "I'll try the disguise," I said. "But if I don't look convincing, I refuse to leave the ship."

Motor Oil, Aspirin, and Minivan gathered around me. While Aspirin smeared pale blue makeup on my skin, Motor Oil glued a fake auxiliary antenna to my scalp and a tiny blue remote-control chip to my fingernail. "Ours are surgically implanted under our fingernails," he explained apologetically, "but I'm not sure how to pry your nail off."

"That's okay," I said quickly. "This will be fine."

Meanwhile, Minivan helped me into a lime-green and lavender jogging suit and slipped gorilla-sized athletic shoes stuffed with empty potato chip bags onto my feet. Then they all stepped back and looked me over.

"Incredible!" Minivan exclaimed.

"Yes," Motor Oil agreed. "What a difference."

Aspirin nodded. "You look very handsome, Russell."

I walked into the bathroom and gazed at myself in the mirror. The boy who looked back at me was a slightly thinner, brown-eyed version of Minivan. "Handsome?" I said under my breath. "I look grotesque—and almost exactly like a Xarabibblian."

"So will you do it?" Minivan asked, poking his head into

the bathroom. "Will you come with us?"

What could I say? I was scared stiff, but at the same time I was tingling with curiosity. There was an entire alien planet out there just waiting to be explored. How could I return to Earth without having experienced it firsthand? Besides, I had come to X-10 to help Minivan and his family. I couldn't back out now, even if it meant flirting with danger, death, and sand fleas.

"I'll do it," I said.

The aliens let out an ecstatic cheer and headed for the door. The TV heroes ran after them.

"Wait!" I shouted. "Captain Spotless, Lady Bug, Chauncy, Stickky Elves, you have to stay on the ship for just one more minute. The Xarabibblians are preparing a feast of grime, sand fleas, Prime Cut, and gift wrap for you, and it would be very impolite to go out until it's ready."

"Who cares about polite?" the Captain bellowed. "I want a toilet to clean, and I want it now!"

"Just sixty seconds," I promised. "You can time us." I grabbed my backpack, ran out the door, and slammed it behind me. I could hear the TV creatures shouting and banging against the door, but I ignored them and engaged the manual airlock. Then I looked around.

"Over here," Minivan called.

He and his parents were climbing up a ladder that led to the top of the stone wall. I joined them and began to climb. A persistent sound—sort of a roaring, wailing, screeching noise—filled my ears.

"What's that?" I shouted over the din.

"The wind blowing the sand around," Minivan shouted back.

The aliens reached the highest rung of the ladder and

scrambled over the top of the wall. I followed and took my first step onto the surface of Xarabibble-10.

Instantly a gale of sand blew in my face. Granules of coarse sand stuck to my blue makeup, filled my nostrils and ears, and coated my tongue.

"Well, what do you think?" Motor Oil asked.

"I can't open my eyes!" I moaned.

"Oops! We forgot you don't have the proper fashion accessories," Aspirin replied. "Here, put these on."

She reached into her pocket and handed me a pair of goggles, some earplugs, and a clothespin. I put the goggles over my eyes, stuck the plugs in my ears, and put the clothespin on my nose. "What about my mouth?" I shouted, struggling to breathe something other than sand.

"Turn up the collar of your jogging suit and pull the drawstring tight," Minivan instructed. "And stop talking."

"Just one more thing," I yelled. "How far away is your hut?"

"Not too far," Motor Oil shouted back. "We can get there in the time it takes to watch fifteen flashies."

I let out a sigh of relief. In fifteen minutes or less we'd be out of the sandstorm. Of course, we'd be sitting in a stone hut full of rude, stinky barbarians. Still, compared to inhaling sand, it sounded pretty good.

"So what now?" I hollered. "Did the underground leave you a Jeep or something?"

Aspirin laughed. "We don't have motor vehicles on X-10. Well, there are a couple of forklifts to unload A-V receivers, but the workers from X-6 keep them locked up."

"Then how are we going to get to your hut?" I screamed.

"Simple," Minivan replied. "We're going to walk."

Chapter
14

"**S**pace exploration is a highly overrated activity!" I hollered as I staggered through the sand behind Minivan and his parents. "In fact, it stinks!"

"What?" Minivan screamed, dodging one of the eight zillion bright orange spiny chucka plants that dotted the landscape.

"Never mind!" I shouted, stumbling over my huge clown sneakers and landing face-first in the sand. Minivan stopped to help me up. I had fallen at the foot of a huge, metallic windmill. It was one of hundreds that stretched out to the horizon like enormous spinning scarecrows. According to Minivan, the X-6 scientists had built them to harness the planet's incredible wind power. The power was then turned into electricity which ran the aliens' beloved A-V receivers.

"How much longer?" I yelled into Minivan's ear.

"Eight, maybe ten flashies' time," he told me, leading me around the windmill.

I groaned, trying to ignore the sand crunching between my molars. "Keep walking!" I bellowed.

We continued on. A chilly wind blew my hair straight back and made my jogging suit ripple against my goosebumped skin. Sand whirled around me, blocking out most of the light that Xarabibble-10's two suns provided. It worked its way into my clothes, behind my goggles, and between my lips. With each step, my oversized shoes grew heavier and heavier.

And then there were the sand fleas. They were ten times as big as Earth fleas and one hundred times as hungry. They leaped all over me, chomping my flesh. Within minutes, I was itching from the top of my fake antenna to the bottoms of my blue feet.

Minivan and his parents, on the other hand, didn't seem to be bothered by the fleas. In fact, the aliens were really good at catching them in midleap. Then they would pop the insects into their mouths and chew happily.

My thoughts drifted back to Earth. I thought about my neighborhood—the green lawns, the blue sky, the warm golden sun. I remembered a couple of days ago when I'd told my mother I might go down to the park and rent some Rollerblades. Of course, I had been lying. Back then, Rollerblading in the park had seemed like the most boring activity in the world.

Now it sounds like heaven, I thought. *The sun shining on my face, almost normal-sized shoes on my feet, and most of all, no sand fleas.*

Minivan's voice broke into my daydream. "Look, there's our hut!" he shouted.

I followed his pointing finger to what looked like some gray lumps on the horizon. The aliens broke into a run and I did my best to follow.

Five minutes and twelve tumbles into the sand later, I stood beside Motor Oil, Aspirin, and Minivan at the edge of X-10 civilization. Hundreds of stone huts, each about the size of a small gas station, dotted the desert in every direction. The huts appeared to have no windows or doors. They all looked exactly alike. "Is this one of your biggest cities?" I shouted.

"This is our *only* city," Minivan yelled back. "Everybody on Xarabibble-10 lives here."

"We used to live in small villages of ten or fifteen huts," Motor Oil explained, "but then the X-6 scientists built the windmills and a power station so we could all have A-V receivers. Naturally, we all moved near the power station where the reception is best."

"We're a small but thriving planet," Aspirin added. "Or at least we were until the barbarians invaded. According to the last census, there are one thousand sixteen Xarabibblians on X-10—and five thousand A-V receivers."

Motor Oil led us to the twelfth hut down, twenty-ninth from the left. "The Home Improvement Depot has everything you need to turn your home into a castle!" he said in a perky announcer's voice. Then his face fell. "Unfortunately, our home is more like a jail cell since the Praxboxians arrived."

"But soon it will be ours again," Aspirin said, patting her husband's shoulder.

Minivan nodded. "Thanks to Captain Spotless, Lady Bug, Chauncy, the Stickky Elves—and our friend Russell."

I was just about to say something suitably modest when suddenly a section of the hut's wall began to move. I jumped back as a slab of rock slid out from the bottom of the hut, revealing a small opening about three feet high and three feet wide. I looked down at the opening and let out a strangled yelp. A Praxboxian barbarian was staring up at me!

How can I describe the face that gazed at me through the gloom? Minivan had told me the barbarians were ugly, hairy, and smelly, but I knew now he had been trying to spare me the full truth. This barbarian had tiny, bloodshot eyes, a nose like a bruised mango, lips like squashed slugs, and fangs like a warthog. His hair was more like fur—long, matted, black-and-white fur that made him look a little like a mutant border collie.

And then there was his odor. It was kind of like moldy broccoli, three-day old-soiled baby diapers, and sour milk all mixed together and sprinkled with skunk spray. And that wasn't even taking into account his bad breath.

The barbarian squinted up at us and let out an ear-splitting roar. Then he reached out with a huge, hairy, clawlike hand, grabbed me by the ankle, and dragged me into the hut.

I was so frightened, I forgot to breathe. *He's going to crush me like an empty can of Zipsi-Cola,* I thought. Instead, he picked me up and stood me on my feet. I gazed up at him, my knees knocking together like castanets. He was so tall that his hairy head brushed against the ceiling.

"Snorp *tengo hambre!*" he croaked. "Get Snorp snack food! *Now!*"

I was so freaked out, it didn't even occur to me to be surprised that the barbarian was speaking in two different Earth languages. All I was thinking about was obeying his order so he wouldn't kill me. I pulled off my goggles, earplugs, and clothespin and shoved them into my pocket. My eyes flitted left and right, frantically searching for a kitchen or a refrigerator or a cabinet—anything that might contain food. In the process, I managed to get a quick look at my surroundings.

I was standing in a small, windowless room, about six feet wide and ten feet long, with a small stone fireplace in the corner. One wall was covered with A-V receivers, all broadcasting Earth flashies from around the planet. On one set an announcer was talking with a British accent; on another I saw a Japanese family singing about rice. One of the receivers was broadcasting nothing but static and snow.

Three more enormous, stinky barbarians were sprawled on the floor in the middle of the room, staring at the A-V receivers. The creatures were surrounded by piles of empty soda cans, shredded potato chip bags, and crushed cookie boxes. As I stared at them in amazement and horror, a Spotless Cleanser commercial appeared on one of the sets.

"Spotless!" one of them roared.

"Wunderbar! Mi piace! Way cool!" the others thundered.

The barbarians bounced up and down, chomped noisily on huge fistfuls of chocolate-covered pretzels, and drooled. Whenever Captain Spotless did something that pleased them, they pointed at the receiver and laughed a raucous "Har! Har! Har!"

Meanwhile, Motor Oil, Aspirin, and Minivan had crawled into the hut. "Greetings, handsome and noble Praxboxians!" Motor Oil called as the flashie ended. "We, your loyal and willing slaves, have returned."

The barbarians turned from the A-V receivers and squinted at us. *"Chi egli?"* demanded one of them, a

103

blubbery creature with a beer belly and mostly black hair. I gulped. He was pointing at me.

"This is my cousin," Minivan said. "His name is, uh . . . uh . . ."

"Deodorant," I said. I guess it was wishful thinking since I was almost suffocating from the smell of barbarian body odor.

"He was living on X-6," Aspirin added, "but we brought him back with us to serve you."

"Yes, uh, sorry we were gone so long," Motor Oil said with fake cheerfulness, "but it rained on X-6 and we couldn't unload the sand until they finished the beach volleyball championships, and then—"

"Shut up *und* get Snorp root beer!" Snorp croaked.

"Mootie *il wil graag* candy corn!" the blubbery barbarian roared.

"Quarg need Gummi worms!" shouted another, picking up an empty can of soda and heaving it at us.

The smallest barbarian, who appeared to be a mere eight feet tall, scratched his armpit. "Comb Gwiddle's hair!" he growled. He pointed a massive furry finger at me. *"Tu!"*

Instantly the aliens sprang into action. They ran into the next room and reappeared moments later carrying trays of root bear, candy corn, and Gummi worms. They hurried to serve the barbarians, who grabbed the food from the trays, shoved the aliens aside with their elbows, and went back to guffawing noisily at the flashies.

Meanwhile, I was still standing in the middle of the room, too petrified to move. Motor Oil, who had been thrown against the wall by a barbarian elbow, looked up and caught my eye. He pointed to a two-foot-long filthy comb that was lying on one of the A-V receivers and then motioned toward

Gwiddle. He mouthed the words, *Hurry up.*

With my heart thumping in my cars, I walked over and picked up the comb. Then I took a hesitant step toward Gwiddle. He rolled onto his back and flung his huge arms over his head. Sand fleas leaped from his hairy armpits. The stench was overpowering.

"Comb *ou de,*" he grunted.

"Comb what?" I asked uncertainly.

He turned his bloodshot eyes toward me. "Comb!" he growled. "Or *die!*"

I dropped to my knees and quickly set to work.

Eight hours later, I was praying a meteor would collide with Xarabibble-10 and blast it to bits—anything to get me away from the Praxboxian invaders. Throughout the day the barbarians had barely moved from the A-V receivers. Hour after hour, they pointed at the flashies and slapped each other and laughed, all the while scarfing down alien snack food. Sometimes, when they laughed a little too hard, bits of potato chips flew out of their noses.

Once in a while, just to add a little variety, the barbarians had a food fight. Then fistfuls of marshmallows, pretzels, and ice cream would go sailing across the room and squish against the wall, the A-V receivers, or—if I didn't duck fast enough—me. The food fight usually ended when the creatures shook up their soda cans and sprayed the sticky liquid all over each other. Then they fell back onto the floor, roaring with laughter, and ordered us to bring them more food and drink.

"Bring Mookie beer nuts!"

"Hitotsu kudasai!" Gwiddle roared, stamping his stinky feet.

Motor Oil, Aspirin, Minivan, and I ran into the kitchen. I glanced over at my friends. They looked as miserable as I felt. Their backs were bent, their faces were damp with sweat and soda spray, and their jogging suits were covered with bits of food.

"How much longer?" I whispered. I didn't dare say more. Whenever the barbarians caught us talking among ourselves, they pitched bottles of root beer at us.

"Hang in there," Motor Oil whispered back. "They're getting sleepy."

We jogged back into the living room, tromping over greasy potato chip bags and crushed aluminum cans as we went. The barbarians grabbed the packets of beer nuts out of our hands and ripped them open with their teeth. They chomped loudly with their mouths open.

On the A-V receivers, commercials from around the world were playing. Happy consumers in Europe, Africa, Asia, and the Americas ate breakfast cereal, made long-distance calls, and drove luxury cars. It looked like paradise. Of course, compared to life as an alien slave, almost anything would look like paradise—even Planet Earth. *Especially* Planet Earth.

"*Kapaal kornu* Snorp!" the barbarian roared.

"Me, too!" Quarg growled.

"*Tusukele olsogi!*" Gwiddle croaked.

Mookie stamped his feet. "*Nien,* me!"

By now, I knew the routine. Motor Oil, Aspirin, Minivan, and I each grabbed a comb and set to work. Mookie was the closest to me so I knelt down and began combing his blubbery belly. Sand fleas were hopping all over me, using my body as their own personal smorgasbord. I held my breath to keep from gagging, and willed myself not to scratch.

And then I noticed something. Mookie's eyes were growing heavy. I glanced over at Snorp, Quarg, and Gwiddle. Their hairy eyelids were drooping shut. Snorp's breathing was deep and steady.

Softly, Motor Oil began to sing: "Take a break with Slumberland Tea, put up your feet, and stack some Z's . . ."

We all joined in: "Drink Slumberland, Slumberland, Slumberland, Slumberland Tea."

Mookie's eyes rolled back in his head. He began to snore and the others joined in. It was like standing in the middle of four chainsaws stuck in high gear. Not that I was complaining. In fact, I felt like jumping for joy.

Motor Oil caught my eye and put his finger to his lips. Slowly, silently, he tiptoed toward the tiny front door and carefully pushed the rock outward. Then he dropped to his knees and crawled outside. Aspirin, Minivan, and I followed.

Instantly, we were back in a world of gale-force winds and swirling sand. The only difference was that now it was nighttime and X-10's four moons—three about the size of our Earth moon, and one almost three times as large—were shining. I zipped up the collar of my jogging suit, put on my goggles, earplugs, and clothespin, and groped for Minivan.

"How long will they sleep?" I shouted.

"A long time," he yelled back. "Through hundreds and hundreds of flashies."

I let out a huge sigh of relief. "What now?"

"We have to get back to the spaceship for our meeting with the underground," Minivan said in my ear. "Come on."

I grabbed his arm, pulled off my jumbo shoes, and started walking. Despite the sandy wind whistling through my teeth, I wanted to talk. It had been hours since we'd been able to speak and I was exploding with emotion.

"That was the worst day of my entire life!" I bellowed.

"Look on the bright side," Minivan shouted back. "At least they didn't figure out you're not really from X-6."

"That's because they were too busy stuffing their faces with junk food and spraying each other with Zipsi-Cola." I scratched one of my four thousand flea bites. "I'd rather cut my wrists with a rusty bean-dip lid than spend another moment combing their stinky armpits."

"Now you understand why we traveled across the universe to beg for your help," Minivan said. "We're desperate."

"Are there Praxboxians living in every hut on X-10?" I asked.

"Yes. They're even forcing us to build more huts so more of their kind can come here."

I tripped over a spiny chucka and stumbled into Minivan. "Why do they talk in all those different languages?" I asked.

"As you saw, we receive flashies from all over your planet," he explained. "The inhabitants of X-10 have learned to speak dozens of Earth languages, but the barbarians have only picked up a few words from their favorite flashies."

"What does their native language sound like?" I asked.

"It's all growls and roars and grunts," he told me, "plus a lot of body language, like throwing things and smacking each other—and us."

"So I noticed."

We walked on through the darkness. My stomach growled and I felt weak, probably because I hadn't eaten anything since dinner with my parents the night before. Back at the aliens' hut I'd been tempted to sneak a few bites of alien snack food, but the thought of what the barbarians might do if they caught me had stopped me. Besides, each time I considered sampling X-10 food, I reminded myself that it was made from processed sand fleas. A fact like that could make anyone want to go on a diet.

Despite the wind and the sand and my empty stomach, I was feeling pretty good. I guess it was because I was no longer breathing barbarian body odor. Plus, I was beginning to get the hang of traveling across the X-10 terrain without inhaling sand, tripping on spiny chucka plants, or slamming into windmills.

"I think I'm learning to like your planet," I shouted at Minivan. "But you need more indoor spaces where you can get away from the sandstorms. Maybe a community center or a museum or a library, and enclosed passageways between the buildings."

"We don't know how to build stuff like that," he screamed in my ear.

"No, but the X-6 scientists probably do. Maybe they'd build you something in return for more sand."

"Maybe. Look," Minivan shouted, pointing to a dim, shimmering light a hundred yards in front of us. "There it is!"

I grabbed his arm and we hurried on. As we got closer to the landing pad, I saw Motor Oil and Aspirin emerging from the darkness ahead of us.

The other members of the underground were arriving, too. There must have been about two dozen of them, all dressed in brightly colored jogging suits and enormous sneakers. When they spotted Motor Oil, Aspirin, and Minivan, they froze and let out a collective shriek. Then they began jumping up and down and talking a mile a minute in Xarabibblian.

"They can't believe we made it back from Earth," Minivan explained to me. "No one has ever left X-10 before except to go to X-6, and that's practically next door."

Motor Oil pointed at me. The aliens stared, their mouths

hanging open despite the whirling sand. I smiled uneasily and waved. I wasn't used to being the center of attention.

"Russell," they chanted. "Russell, Russell, Russell."

They gathered around me, their eyes wide. Two or three of them reached out and gingerly touched my skin. The blue makeup I was wearing came off on their fingers. They gasped and exchanged astonished looks.

"What's going on?" I asked.

"They've never seen a real live Earthling before," Minivan explained. "Besides, you're a celebrity."

Motor Oil and Aspirin climbed down the stairs that led to the landing pad. The other members of the underground followed. Minivan and I brought up the rear. We gathered outside the door of the spaceship and waited. I wasn't sure what we were waiting for, but I noticed the aliens kept sneaking looks at me.

I grinned nervously. Maybe I was supposed to do something, like quote a commercial or something. Or maybe it was up to me to start the meeting. The thought made my palms sweat. I wiped them on my jogging suit, leaving pale blue streaks on the fabric.

Just as I was about to lean over and ask Minivan for help, the door of the spaceship flew open and an enormously fat Xarabibblian in a pure white jogging suit stepped out. Rolls of bluish white flesh hung from his chin, and the zipper on the front of his jogging suit looked as if it was about to burst from the strain of holding in his huge stomach.

"It's our beloved chief," Motor Oil whispered in my ear.

The crowd drew back as he walked toward us. He stopped in front of Motor Oil and looked him up and down.

"So, Citizen Motor Oil," said the Honorable Dental Floss,

an expression of disbelief on his blubbery face, "you actually flew to Earth and lived to tell about it."

"Yes, and we found Russell, who helped us bring back Captain Spotless, Lady Bug, Chauncy, and the Stickky Elves," Motor Oil said proudly. "Our heroes are in the ship, as you no doubt saw for yourself, awaiting Russell's command to defeat the barbarian invaders."

"Well, well, well," said Dental Floss, still looking slightly amazed. "Good job."

"Thank you, illustrious leader," Motor Oil said. "Any loyal Xarabibblian would have done the same."

"Yes, yes," Dental Floss said with a wave of his hand. He turned to me. "And you are Russell." He stuck out his fat, fleshy hand.

I shook his hand and cleared my throat. Meeting new people always made me nervous. And this wasn't just any new person—this was the leader of an entire alien planet. "Uh, pleased to meet you," I muttered, shuffling my feet.

The chief gave me a hearty pat on the back. "You're always welcome at the Beddy-Bye Motel!" he exclaimed in a booming voice.

"Th-the Beddy-Bye," I stammered shyly, "where you . . . uh . . . you enter as a stranger and leave as a friend."

The chief grinned and the aliens let out a cheer. I allowed myself to breathe again. Apparently I'd said the right thing. I managed a lopsided smile.

"Friends," Dental Floss proclaimed, gazing out at the crowd, "Motor Oil and his family have returned. Now I have the honor of presenting you with Earth Citizen Russell, who will introduce our flashie heroes and then tell us his plans for leading them into battle against the barbarian hordes!"

My smile shrunk like a wool sweater in a hot dryer. "Um . . . er," I stammered. Didn't these aliens realize I was an introvert? It said so right on my report card. I could barely give an oral report in front of my classmates, let alone a speech to the entire Xarabibblian underground.

Besides, what was I supposed to say to the aliens? Should I tell them that their hero, the amazing Captain Spotless, was actually a cleanliness drill sergeant with about as much warmth as an iceberg? That Lady Bug was vain, Chauncy was sarcastic, and the Stickky Elves were a bunch of brats?

Somehow I didn't think the aliens wanted to hear any of that. And I was absolutely positive they didn't want to know that the barbarians scared me silly. Or that I really didn't have any plan at all, except to point out the barbarians to the TV creatures and hope that when the dust cleared, the Praxboxians would be on the run.

While I was thinking all this, the crowd began to chant. "Tell us, Russell!" they cried. "Tell us, tell us, tell us!"

Someone lifted me up onto the ladder. I gazed down at the crowd, which immediately fell silent. I could feel beads of sweat popping out on my forehead. My hands were shaking and my knees were weak. "Gee . . . um . . . er . . . " I squeaked. "Uh, hi there,"

Get a grip, Russell, I told myself. You sound like an imbecile.

I opened my mouth, but all that came out was more of the same. "Uh . . . er . . . well," I blathered. "I . . . uh . . ."

My voice trailed off. The aliens' colorful jogging suits blurred before my eyes. Then the colors started to spin like a pinwheel in a hurricane. I blinked once, twice . . . then everything went black.

≫ Chapter ≪

16

hen I woke up, I was lying on the floor of the spaceship. Motor Oil, Aspirin, and Minivan were gathered around me.

"When you're under the weather, let Weatherwell's Cough Drops soothe your aching throat," Minivan said, patting my arm.

"Stop that burning itch with Rash-Away," Aspirin added. "Proven effective in nine out of ten cases."

Motor Oil nodded. "It's the one recommended by doctors."

I let out a low groan. I knew the aliens were trying to be nice, but I was in no mood to quote flashies. "Get me my backpack," I said.

Minivan jumped up and returned with it a moment later. I ripped it open and pulled out three cans of Prime Cut Dog Food, my toothbrush, and the spare pair of socks and underwear I had packed before we left Earth. I tossed them aside and kept looking. At the bottom of the pack I found what I was after—a box of granola bars I'd taken from the pantry back home.

I grabbed a granola bar, yanked it out of the wrapper, and chewed it up. Then I ate another, and another. Slowly I was starting to feel almost normal. "What happened?" I asked.

"You fainted," Motor Oil said.

"You've been out cold most of the night," Minivan added. "We tried to wake you, but you wouldn't budge."

That's when I realized that until I fainted I hadn't slept a wink since I left Earth over thirty-six hours ago. "I guess I was tired," I said. "And hungry, too." I looked around the ship. "Where did everyone go?"

"The chief had to return home," Aspirin explained. "His house is closely guarded and it's very difficult and dangerous for him to slip away. He only came because he wanted to meet the hero who is going to save our planet."

Some hero, I thought. *I passed out in front of the entire Xarabibblian underground.*

"Everyone else is still outside, waiting to see if you're all right," Aspirin said. "Maybe you'd better go talk to them."

I shook my head. "I'm not good at public speaking. Large groups of people—er, I mean aliens—give me stage fright."

"Don't be silly," Minivan chuckled. "You talk to tons of people on the Internet."

"But that's different. All I do is sit in my bedroom and type words on a computer screen. The real people are miles and miles away."

"But it's almost dawn and the barbarians will be waking up soon," Motor Oil insisted. "You must tell us when you plan to launch your attack and what our role in the battle will be."

Minivan grabbed my arm. "Xarabibble-10 awaits your orders."

I gazed into Minivan's sort of purple eyes and tried to

think. What had I gotten myself into? The aliens thought I was some sort of hero—one step down from Captain Spotless. And I had let them believe it. In fact, for a while there they had almost convinced me.

But that was before we landed on X-10. Back on Planet Earth, this whole trip had seemed like a fun fantasy—a sort of *Star Trek* rerun come to life. Now things seemed a lot more real, and a heck of a lot more dangerous. I mean, the Praxboxian invaders were rude and violent even when they were happy. I sure as heck didn't want to be around to see how they would react if something—or someone—made them really mad.

"Listen," I began hesitantly, "about this battle stuff. Maybe we should wait a few days and think things over. I mean, the barbarians aren't really such bad guys. Maybe we could work out a compromise—you know, like we could offer them an autographed photo of Captain Spotless and his buddies in return for your freedom."

Motor Oil looked at me strangely. "He's delirious," he said.

"Give him another granola bar," Aspirin suggested.

"Speaking of Captain Spotless," Minivan broke in, "where is he?"

I frowned. "What do you mean, where is he?"

"I mean, we left him in the spaceship along with Lady Bug, Chauncy, and the Stickky Elves, right?" Minivan said, his voice rising. "But now they're not here. So where are they?"

"Okay, let's not panic," I said, panic-stricken. "You must have seen them when you brought me into the ship after I fainted, right?"

"Uh, come to think of it, no," Aspirin admitted.

I threw my hands in the air and let out a groan. "Those TV commercial cretins! They must have escaped while we were at your hut." I kicked my backpack across the ship. "Some superheroes! They've been nothing but trouble since we zapped them out of the TV."

"What are we going to do?" Minivan asked in a small voice.

"We're going to find them," I said firmly. "And when we do, I'm going to give them a piece of my mind. I'm sick of playing nursemaid to a bunch of cartoons." I jumped to my feet and headed for the door. "Come on."

Outside the ship, the alien underground was waiting for us. Without even stopping to think, I pushed my way through the crowd, climbed halfway up the ladder, and shouted, "Captain Spotless, Lady Bug, Chauncy, and the Stickky Elves are missing!"

A gasp went up from the crowd. Then they began jabbering away in Xarabibblian.

"Quiet!" I cried. To my amazement, they obeyed. "If my hunch is right, the TV heroes left the ship and got lost in the sand and the wind," I said. "Now it's up to us to find them. I want all of you to climb out of the landing pad and form a circle around it. Then start walking away from the ship. Keep your eyes peeled. If you spot the Captain or any of the others, hurry back and tell me." I paused, giving them a moment to take it all in. "Okay," I commanded, "move out!"

The Xarabibblians sprung into action. They climbed the ladder, formed a circle around the ship, and headed off across the desert in search of Captain Spotless and his buddies.

"I thought you said you weren't any good at public speaking," Minivan remarked as the aliens disappeared.

"I'm not."

"Well, you handled that situation pretty well," he said. "In fact, you were awesome!"

I thought it over. Minivan was right. I *had* done okay. I guess I'd been so angry at Captain Spotless and his buddies that I hadn't had time to get nervous. I smiled. Maybe there was a touch of the hero in me after all.

"Earth Citizen Russell!" called a voice from the darkness. "Come quick!"

I pulled up my collar and followed an alien in a pink-and-black jogging suit. Minivan and his parents came, too. We hadn't gone far before we found the cartoon characters huddled together at the base of a windmill, half-buried in sand.

"Hey, it's me, Russell!" I called as I ran up. "Are you all right?"

"Oh, we're just swell," Chauncy answered. "It's always been my dream to be simultaneously devoured by fleas *and* buried alive."

"I *told* you not to leave the ship," I said irritably.

"We were bored," whined the elf named Bert. "When the fat guy in the white suit showed up, we left to find something to tape."

A fat guy in a white suit. That could only mean the chief. But why hadn't he told me that the TV creatures had escaped? It didn't make sense.

"Yeah, but our tape doesn't work here," Bo said. "It gets covered with sand the second we unroll it."

"Now listen, you crybabies," I began. "It's time you stopped complaining and started—"

"I hate this lousy planet!" Captain Spotless interrupted. "I can barely shoot my superpowered soap bubbles in all this wind and sand, and I can't fly straight."

"You think y*ou've* got it bad," Lady Bug wailed. "There are fleas everywhere, but when I try to spray them, the wind blows my BugBeGone back into my face!"

"I'm fed up!" Captain Spotless roared, stamping his feet. "Put me back in the TV or I'll scrub your tonsils with a toothbrush!"

By now, most of the Xarabibblians had found us. They were gathered around us, staring at the cartoon creatures with a combination of awe, fear, and confusion. No doubt they were wondering why the stars of their favorite flashies—the superheroes who were supposed to save their planet—were pouting like a bunch of spoiled kindergartners.

"Russell, look," Minivan whispered, stepping up beside me and pointing skyward.

I followed his gaze. The four moons of X-10 were fading from the sky and the planet's two suns were rising on opposite horizons. And that's when it hit me—a plan. Or at least sort of an idea.

In the reruns of old Westerns I had watched on TV, the Indians always attacked at dawn. That's because it gave them the advantage of surprise. By the time the cowboys woke up and pulled their pants on, the Indians had already shot a few dozen burning arrows into their roofs.

Why shouldn't we do the same? Not the burning arrows part, of course, but the element of surprise. I mean, how dangerous could the Praxboxians be when they were half-asleep and probably sick to their stomachs from scarfing too much junk food? With a little luck, we could drive them off the planet and be back on Earth in time for a late lunch.

Okay, okay, so maybe I was being a little optimistic. But somehow, standing there in the middle of nowhere with the X-10 underground gazing at me like I was the answer to their prayers, it all seemed to make sense. Besides, I was so sick of baby-sitting Captain Spotless and his buddies I felt like screaming. It was time those TV twits got off their self-centered butts and did something useful. And I knew just how to make it happen.

"Captain Spotless, Lady Bug, Chauncy, Bo, Binky, Bill, and Bert, listen up!" I announced. "I know this trip hasn't been much fun for you so far, but all that is about to change."

"It couldn't get any worse, that's for sure," Chauncy muttered, flicking sand out of his eyes with his paws.

I ignored him. "First, I'm going to take you out of the sand and wind. Second, I'm going to introduce you to the dirtiest, smelliest, most flea-infested creatures in the entire universe." I turned to the Captain. "Captain Spotless," I said, "you are the only super-hero powerful enough to get these disgusting creatures clean."

"Darn right!" he thundered.

"Lady Bug, no one but you could charm their many fleas and then blast them to kingdom come."

"You got *that* right, big boy," she cooed.

I turned to the elves. "And only the Stickky Elves have tape strong enough to wrap around the creatures' greasy, filthy fur."

"You know it!" the elves exclaimed in their munchkin voices.

"Hey, what's in it for me?" Chauncy demanded.

"When you see these smelly beasts," I said, "I want you to go for the throat. Each time you land a bite, I'll give you a can of Prime Cut."

Chauncy eyed me skeptically. "Why should I believe you? I haven't had one can of Prime Cut since we landed on this dreadful ball of sand, and I'm wasting away."

"Yeah," said Bo. "All you've done is lie to us. Why should we do anything for you?"

It was time to bring out the big guns. "Because if you don't," I replied, "I won't put you back inside the television. What's more, I'll leave you on Xarabibble-10 forever."

Captain Spotless lunged forward, grabbed me by the front

of my jogging suit, and dangled me in the air. "If you don't send me back where I came from," he roared, "I'll wring you out like a dirty dishrag!"

My heart was pounding so hard I was sure it was about to crash through my rib cage, but I forced my voice to remain quiet and calm. "If you hurt me," I said, "then I *definitely* won't be able to put you back inside the TV. In fact, if I were you, I'd be very, very nice to me."

"Why?" Chauncy demanded.

"Because I'm the only person in the entire universe who knows how to program the spaceship to return to Earth. Furthermore, only I know how to use the quantum-particle pattern-recognition box that brought you here. That means I'm the only one who knows how to send you back."

I was bluffing, of course. Getting us back to Earth was no problem, but zapping the commercial characters back into the TV was another matter. I wasn't even positive the pattern-recognition box would work in reverse. In any case, the X-6 scientists knew much more about the process than I did. But luckily, the cartoon creatures didn't know that.

Chauncy let out an exasperated sigh. "Where do we find these revolting creatures you want me to sink my teeth into?" he asked.

"Now you're talking!" I exclaimed. "Just follow me. They live in stone huts just a few minutes away from here."

"Well, what in blue blazes are we waiting for?" the Captain bellowed. "Let's go find them!"

The aliens let out a cheer. Trying to ignore the nagging feeling that I had absolutely no idea what I was doing, I turned and started off across the sand in search of the barbarian hordes.

Chapter

17

It wasn't long before the Xarabibblians' drab stone huts came into view. Inside the huts, hundreds and hundreds of hairy, smelly barbarians lay blissfully sleeping. Soon they would be yawning, stretching, calling out for snack food—and crushing their slaves' pathetic little skulls if they didn't get it.

It was about then that the reality of what I was doing sunk in. I, Russell Brinkerhoff, TV commercial junkie and proven shy person, was on an alien planet, light-years from home, about to lead a war against a race of creatures who could pulverize the entire World Wrestling Federation.

"This is insane!" I cried, waving my arms. "Retreat! Retreat!"

But no one was listening. The wind was roaring, the Xarabibblian underground was cheering, and Captain Spotless, Lady Bug, Chauncy, and the elves were running toward the nearest hut like a football team driving for the goalposts.

Unfortunately, when they got there they had no idea how to get inside. They stopped, stared, and shouted. Captain Spotless kicked the wall. The members of the underground (who had stopped and were watching warily from about one hundred feet away) began calling out instructions—something about kneeling down and grabbing the almost invisible bottom edge of the small stone door—but with everyone yelling at once it was impossible to make sense of what they were saying.

I stood at the back of the crowd, wondering whether to help or to dig a hole in the sand, climb in it, and hope the barbarians would mistake me for a large sand flea. Before I could decide, the stone door fell open and the hugest, foulest-smelling barbarian I had ever seen stuck his head out. He blinked, yawned, and rubbed his eyes.

The Xarabibblians drew back and cowered. "It's Hork, the barbarian chief!" I heard someone cry.

Hork looked at Chauncy and his powerful jaw dropped. He frowned, shook his head, and looked again. Then his mouth twisted into something that might have been a smile. "You dog from flashies," he said with amazement. "You Chauncy!"

Chauncy responded by lunging forward and biting Hork on the nose.

"Yow!" the barbarian howled. He held his nose and stared at Chauncy in astonishment. Then he disappeared back inside the hut.

"I say, did you see that?" Chauncy proclaimed, turning toward the crowd. "I was quite all right, wasn't I?"

The Xarabibblians let out a triumphant cheer and my heart lifted. Maybe we weren't going to be massacred after all. I mean, if one little nip on the nose was enough to scare the barbarian chief back into his hut, just think what a blast of Captain Spotless's superpowered soap bubbles would do.

I reached into my backpack and held up a can of Prime Cut. "Go get 'em, Chauncy! Your reward is waiting!"

Chauncy wagged his tail and trotted into the hut. "Hey, wait for me!" Captain Spotless roared happily, dropping to his knees. "Those animals are filthy!"

"And covered with fleas," Lady Bug purred, tossing her hair over her shoulder. The elves circled around her, giggling eagerly.

Suddenly there was a loud bark and Chauncy came sailing back out through the door. He slammed into the Captain, who fell backward into Lady Bug. All three of them hit the sand with a thud, almost squashing the elves in the process.

"Get off me, you lughead!" Lady Bug shrieked, shoving the Captain with her four arms. He rolled onto Binky Elf, who squealed like a mouse caught in a trap.

The cause of all this confusion was Hork, who was crawling out of the hut backward and had apparently slammed Chauncy with his enormous foot. The barbarian chief was followed by three other Praxboxians. When they stood up, my heart sank. Compared to the barbarians, Lady Bug and Chauncy looked insignificant, and even Captain Spotless seemed kind of puny. As for the elves—well, they were about as threatening as dust balls.

After the barbarians crawled out, three confused-looking Xarabibblians—the owners of the hut who were now the barbarians' slaves—poked their heads out the door. They stared with fear and bafflement at the flashies characters, the two dozen members of the Xarabibblian underground, and me.

Somehow I felt I should say something. After all, I was supposed to be in charge. "Um . . . er, hello there. My name is Russell, and uh . . . I've come from Planet Earth with Captain Spotless, Lady Bug, Chauncy, and the Stickky Elves to free the Xarabibblian slaves. So, um . . . I would suggest that you Praxboxians go back to your own planet now. Otherwise . . . well, I'm afraid we're going to have to hurt you."

Nobody moved. Nobody spoke. Then Hork pointed at Chauncy, turned to his fellow barbarians, and said, "*Voila!* What did I tell you? *Esta* Chauncy."

"And Captain Spotless!" another barbarian exclaimed.

"Lady Bug!" the third shouted.

"The Stickky Elves!" cried the fourth.

They laughed loudly, spraying foul-smelling saliva everywhere, and shoved each other with delight.

Then Hork plopped down in the sand. "Do stuff!" he commanded, waving his clawlike hand toward the TV characters. "Make flashies—*ahora!* Now!"

Captain Spotless merely smiled and rubbed his hands together. "You are the most dirty, filthy, unhygienic beast I have ever laid eyes on!" he bellowed. "I'm going to enjoy this!"

Then everything seemed to happen at once. The Captain let loose a massive blast of superpowered soap bubbles. Despite the swirling wind, they flew at Hork and smacked him right in the face.

Meanwhile, Lady Bug jumped onto Hork's back and began spraying BugBeGone in his ear. At the same time, the elves were crawling up Hork's legs. They wrapped Stickky tape around his knees one, two, three times, giggling all the while.

Chauncy was busy, too. He ran around Hork, growling and

snapping. He jumped up and landed a bite on the barbarian chief's ear, then turned to look at me. "I hope you're watching because I'm getting hungry!" he called.

It was about then that the Praxboxian invaders realized what we had already figured out—dealing with TV commercial characters up close and personal was not half as much fun as watching them on A-V receivers. The barbarians, however, reacted a lot more strongly—and violently—than we did.

"*Zoot alors!*" Hork cried, rubbing soap bubbles out of his eyes. "Dat stings!" He stood up, which caused the Stickky tape around his knees to snap like a dried-up rubber band. Then he shook his leg. Squealing elves flew in every direction.

Captain Spotless reared back, ready to shoot another blast of soap bubbles. But before he could let loose, Hork stepped forward and shoved him in the chest. The Captain flew backward and landed on his rear end in the sand.

"Ow!" he wailed, pointing at Hork. "He pushed me! He pushed me!" Then Captain Spotless burst into tears.

Next, Hork reached down and grabbed Chauncy by the tail. The barbarian spun the poor mutt over his head like a cowboy twirling a lasso, then let him loose. Chauncy flew a good hundred feet and landed on a spiny chucka.

"*Aah-oooh!*" he howled. He rolled gingerly off the chucka plant and lay there with his tail between his legs, whimpering.

Now the only one left was Lady Bug. She was still wrapped around Hork's back, spraying BugBeGone in his face. One of the other barbarians reached out to pull her off, but Hork held up his hand. "What dat smell?" he growled. "BugBeGone!" he roared with delight. "Mmmm! *Oishii!* Hork like!"

Lady Bug smiled and slid off Hork's back. "Well, well,

well," she purred. "You obviously have good taste. What did you say your name was?"

"Me Hork."

"Ooh," Lady Bug squealed, "I think I'm in love! Come on, you big, bad bundle of barbarian brawn, let's go inside. We've got some serious spraying to do!"

What a disaster! Nothing was turning out the way I'd imagined. Captain Spotless's superpowered soap bubbles, Chauncy's snapping teeth, and the elves' Stickky Adhesive Tape were about as threatening to the barbarians as a squirt gun would be to a charging rhino. And it appeared that to a Praxboxian nose, BugBeGone Bug Spray was a delicate perfume.

To make matters worse, the barbarians in the nearby huts had heard the commotion and were now coming outside to see what was going on. When they saw that the stars of their favorite flashies had somehow materialized right there on X-10—and that their very own barbarian chief was lost in a lip lock with the lovely Lady Bug—they hurried over to get a better look.

And then one of them spotted us.

"*Mira!*" roared a barbarian with black hair and a beer belly. It was Mootie. "Slaves!"

"*Our* slaves!" added Gwiddle, pointing at Motor Oil, Aspirin, and Minivan.

Hork stopped kissing Lady Bug and looked over at the Xarabibblian underground and me. He seemed to be seeing us for the first time. Then he opened his huge mouth and let out a terrifying roar. "*Kele!* Catch them! Then *zabit!* Kill them!"

The barbarians ran back into their huts, probably to get

some sort of horrible alien weapon. I turned to talk over the situation with the underground, but I was a little late. The Xarabibblians were already running off across the sand as fast as their ape-sized feet would carry them.

I knew I should follow them, but something made me hesitate. It was my TV commercial heroes. I just couldn't accept the fact that they had given up so easily. Deep down, I still believed in them.

"Captain Spotless, what's wrong with you?" I shouted, running over to him. "Get up and fight!"

"My chest hurts," he whined. "And look, I got a boo-boo on my finger."

"Stop being such a wimp! Get up and blast the barbarians with your superpowered soap bubbles."

"I don't want to," he pouted, beginning to blubber again. "Those guys don't play fair. They fight back."

I threw up my hands in frustration and ran over to the Stickky Elves, who were huddled at the base of a spiny chucka plant, trying to pick the sand off their tape. "Come on, you guys!" I cried encouragingly. "Get up and tape something!"

They did, but it wasn't what I expected. Instead of running after the barbarians, they scrambled up the inside of my pants legs and taped themselves to the fabric.

"Hey, come out here!" I commanded, struggling to turn my pants legs inside out. They responded by stabbing me with the serrated edge of their tape dispensers. "Ow!" I yelped. "Stop that!"

Zzzzow! I looked up and gasped. The barbarians had reappeared. There must have been fifty of them, all armed with enormous guns, which they were shooting menacingly into the air as they marched toward me. A green laserlike ray flew out of the guns, leaving pale green sparks that crackled as they drifted down to the sand. I wondered what those sparks would do if they touched my skin. Then I changed my mind—I didn't want to know.

Frantically, I looked around for Lady Bug but she was nowhere to be found. Apparently, she had gone inside Hork's hut and the two of them were making beautiful music together with a can of BugBeGone.

That left Chauncy.

"Go on, boy!" I called to him encouragingly. "Sic 'em!"

Chauncy trotted over to my side, and for a moment I thought he was going to obey. Then he growled at me. "Why should I bite those hairy monsters when you're the one with the dog food?" With that, he leaped up and bit my leg.

"Ouch!" one of the elves cried from inside my pants leg.

Zzzzow! The barbarians were blasting their weapons again, only this time they were aiming at me.

"Russell," a familiar voice called, "what are you waiting for? Run! Run!"

I spun around to see Minivan motioning to me from behind a spiny chucka plant. I decided to take his advice. With Chauncy and Captain Spotless at my heels and the Stickky Elves in my pants, I turned and hightailed it across the whirling sand.

⇒ Chapter ⇐

18

inivan and I held hands and ran through the sand like Hansel and Gretel running from the wicked witch. Only in this case, the witch was an army of ten-foot-tall barbarians with deadly ray guns. Captain Spotless and Chauncy jogged behind us, moaning and complaining the whole way.

"My boo-boo is getting sand in it," the Captain shouted over the wind. "I need a Band-Aid!"

"Shut up and keep running!" I yelled back. "If those barbarians catch us, you're going to need a body cast."

"Why in tarnation did that germ-infested palooka push me?" the Captain demanded. "Doesn't he know I'm Captain Spotless?"

"Captain Gutless would be more like it," Chauncy replied.

"Look who's talking!" the Captain bellowed. "You may look like a dog, but you act like a chicken!"

"What do you expect?" Chauncy retorted. "I haven't had my Prime Cut today."

"Is that all you think about?" I cried angrily.

"Yes," he replied. "That and the five hundred pointy things that are sticking in my backside."

"They're spiny chucka needles," Minivan shouted. "Very painful."

"You don't say," Chauncy remarked dryly.

"We'll pull them out when we get to the underground landing pad," Minivan said. He looked over his shoulder. "*If* we get to the underground landing pad."

I followed Minivan's gaze. The only thing I could see behind us was swirling sand. Even the sound of the barbarians' bazookas had faded away. "I think we lost them," I shouted.

"Maybe. The barbarians haven't had much practice traveling through the sand. In fact, they haven't left our huts since they landed on the planet."

"So maybe they gave up and went back to their A-Vs," I said hopefully.

Minivan didn't look convinced. "They're not going to rest until they find us. And when they do . . ."

"Keep running!" I shouted.

When we spotted the dim light that marked the underground landing pad, I felt like shouting for joy. Never before had any place seemed so cozy and inviting. I could hardly wait to climb down the ladder and rest my back against the high stone wall—safe and protected from the wind, the sand, and best of all, the barbarian hordes.

But when I finally climbed down the ladder and looked around, my spirits fell like a battleship anchor. The rest of the underground had already arrived. They lay sprawled on the floor with sand in their hair and sad, dejected looks on their faces. Everything about them seemed to cry out *defeat*.

That's when it really, truly hit me. The Xarabibblians had been counting on me to save their planet, and I had failed. Failed miserably. My sort of plan—to attack at dawn and surprise the barbarians—had been useless. And my attempts to lead Captain Spotless and his buddies into battle had been a joke.

It was almost as if the aliens could read my mind. "We don't blame y*ou*," Motor Oil said glumly.

Aspirin nodded. "The Praxboxians are just too powerful," she said. "Even Captain Spotless couldn't stop them."

"*Couldn't* stop them?" I muttered under my breath. "He didn't even try."

Scowling, I glanced over at my TV commercial heroes. Captain Spotless was holding up his cut finger and scrubbing the ladder with his other hand. Chauncy was plucking chucka needles out of his rear end and whining for Prime Cut. The elves had crawled out of my pants leg and were sticking tape across the door of the spaceship. And Lady Bug? She had deserted us and joined the enemy.

Some heroes! I thought. *They're useless. Absolutely useless.*

But then hadn't I known that almost from the beginning? I didn't want to admit it, but it was true. From the first moment I zapped Captain Spotless and his cohorts out of the TV, I could see they weren't the selfless superheroes I had fantasized about when I was little. How could they be? Even after being blasted with a beam of focused electromagnetic particles, they weren't superheroes, or even human beings. They were cartoons, created by advertising executives like my father to sell products.

Suddenly, all those years I had spent in front of the television seemed like a waste of time. I mean, sure, watching TV is fun—

it always had been and it always would be. But it isn't the real world. And the stuff I'd seen and learned in TV commercials wasn't going to help me solve the real-life problems I was facing now—like how to stop the barbarians from mashing us like a bowl of Mother's Helper Instant Mashed Potatoes.

I looked over at the rest of the underground. They were gazing at me with hope in their eyes. Even now, I felt certain, they didn't want to stop believing in their flashie heroes. In fact, I knew it would only take one encouraging word from me to convince them that Captain Spotless could defeat the barbarians if only he were given another chance.

Naturally, I was tempted to lie and tell my friends that everything was going to be all right. But I couldn't. It just wouldn't be right. Still, I knew I had to do something to help them. But what?

I glanced at Minivan. He was sitting with his mother and father, cleaning sand out of his ears. I thought about the games of tic-tac-toe we had played on the ship, and how Minivan had finally beaten me. If any of the aliens had the smarts to make sense of our situation, it was him. Besides, I needed someone to talk to, and aside from Travis—who was definitely not within shouting distance—Minivan was my best friend.

"Minivan," I said, "can I see you for a minute— inside the ship?"

He jumped up and followed me. I ripped the Stickky tape off the door and we walked inside.

"Do you have a plan?" he asked eagerly.

I sat on the floor and took a deep breath. "I wish I could say yes, but I don't," I admitted. "In fact, I have no idea what to do next."

Minivan dropped down beside me. He looked scared.

"Come on, Russell, this is no time to joke around. When are you and the Captain going to launch your next attack?"

I shook my head. "Face it, Minivan. Captain Spotless and his pals have been nothing but trouble from the moment we met them. If we want to defeat the barbarian hordes, we're going to have to find a way to do it ourselves."

Now Minivan looked downright petrified. "If our flashie heroes can't stop them, how do you expect *us* to do it?"

"We may not be muscle men, but we have something the flashies guys *and* the Praxboxians don't have."

"What's that?"

"Brains," I said. "Somehow we've got to outwit the barbarians. Now, come on, help me think of a way."

Minivan looked skeptical, but he gave it a try. We both sat there in silence, thinking hard. The suddenly, Minivan's face lit up.

"What is it?" I asked. "Do you have an idea?"

"I think we should run away," he announced.

"You mean, leave the planet?"

"That sounds good," he said. "For example, Earth was pretty nice—especially the mall. Can't you take us back home with you?"

"I don't know," I replied uncertainly. "This spaceship only carries about ten passengers at a time, twenty tops. It would take dozens of trips to transport all the Xarabibblians to Earth. Then you'd have to find jobs and places to live, and you'd have to keep your identities secret." I thought back to the day I had taken Minivan and his parents to the mall. They had been about as inconspicuous as a pit bull at a cat show. "I just don't think it would work."

"Well . . . if you say so," he said reluctantly.

We went back to thinking. For some reason, a silly TV commercial my father had created for the Twinkle Toes Foot Massager kept running through my head. In the ad, a pirate steals a shipload of foot massagers supposedly bound for fifteenth-century Spain, and Christopher Columbus sails off to find it. According to the commercial, Columbus never set out to discover the New World; he was just searching for his Twinkle Toes Foot Massager.

I kept trying to figure out what a Twinkle Toes TV commercial had to do with Xarabibble-10. And then suddenly, I made the connection. The commercial was saying that life is so lousy without the Twinkle Toes Foot Massager, people will travel the world to find one.

"What is the barbarians' equivalent of the Twinkle Toes Foot Massager?" I said out loud.

Minivan looked at me as if I had lost my mind. "I don't know."

"The flashies!" I cried. "It's their drug, their pacifier. The Praxboxians can find slave labor and snack food on other planets. It's the flashies that keep them here."

A glimmer of understanding shone in Minivan's eyes. "You mean . . ." he began.

I nodded. "If the flashies transmissions stopped, the barbarians would leave."

Minivan furrowed his brow and bit his lip. He seemed to be struggling with something. Then finally he set his jaw and said, "We're going to have to smash all the A-V receivers."

I stared at Minivan, amazed and impressed. For someone who loved the flashies as much as he did, his suggestion was practically revolutionary. Plus, it took real brain power to come up with it. Unfortunately, it wasn't going to work.

"It's a great idea," I said gently, "but the barbarians are sure to find us before we finish. Any plan we come up with has to be fast and sneaky."

Minivan's face fell. "But how can we turn off the flashies unless we destroy all our receivers?"

"Maybe we don't have to turn off the flashies," I said, thinking out loud. "Maybe we can just redirect them."

"But how?"

"Does anyone on X-10 own a large-screen projection television?"

Minivan nodded. "The chief does. The X-6 scientists gave it to him to mark the first anniversary of our trade agreement."

Slowly the pieces were starting to fall together. "This just might work," I said thoughtfully.

"What might work?" Minivan demanded. "What are you talking about?"

"Of course, I won't know if I've been successful until nightfall," I continued, half to myself. "But I guess it's worth a try. After all, what have I got to lose?"

"Your life?" Minivan suggested.

"Don't remind me," I said. I jumped to my feet and headed for the door. The fate of Xarabibble-10 was in my hands, but somehow I wasn't scared. In fact, I felt strangely happy.

This time, I'm not counting on any TV commercial superheroes, I told myself. *This time, if I succeed, the hero will be me.*

"Russell has a plan!" Minivan announced as we walked out of the ship.

"It's not my plan, it's *our* plan," I said, patting him on the back.

"Tell us!" one of the members of the underground cried.

Once again the chant began. "Tell us, tell us, tell us!"

Minivan opened his mouth, but I held up my hand. I was so focused on what I wanted to say, I didn't even feel nervous. "It's a secret," I said.

"But why?" he asked.

"Why?" the underground chanted. "Why? Why?"

"Because my last plan was a total bomb and I don't want to get everyone's hopes up again," I explained to the crowd. "Besides, if the barbarians happen to find you and question you, I don't want anyone blurting out where we are."

"I hope you don't think *we're* going to get near those barbarian blokes again," Chauncy said. He had found the Prime Cut in my backpack and devoured it. Now he was licking the cans.

"They're bullies," Captain Spotless sniveled.

"And big," Binky Elf squeaked.

"Don't worry," I told them. "This plan doesn't involve anyone except me." I turned to the aliens. "When darkness falls, I want you to look up at the sky. If you see anything unusual, meet me at the chief's hut."

The undergound let out a cheer. "Russell! Russell! Russell!" they chanted.

It was flattering to hear them call my name, but I didn't let it go to my head. I knew I didn't deserve it—not yet, anyway. I turned to Motor Oil, Aspirin, and Minivan. "Can you give me directions to the electrical power station and the chief's hut?"

"Better yet," Motor Oil said, "we can show you."

I shook my head. "I appreciate the offer, but I don't think you understand what we're up against. I mean, this isn't a flashie starring Captain Spotless. This is real life, and it's dangerous."

"That's why we have to come," Aspirin said earnestly. "Russell, you've risked your life to help us and you're not even a Xarabibblian. The least we can do is come with you."

Motor Oil nodded. "Besides, we know the way better than you do. Without our help, you could get lost in a sandstorm."

I thought it over. What good was my brilliant plan if I couldn't find my way to the power plant and the chief's hut? Besides, I might need Motor Oil to help me translate some important instructions.

Then Minivan said something that clinched it. "Russell, you're our friend," he told me. "And friends stick together."

I smiled. Motor Oil, Aspirin, Minivan, and I had been through a lot together. It didn't seem right to leave them behind now. "When friends get together," I said, "they break out the Apple Valley Sparkling Cider."

Minivan grinned. "So take a drink, and take a seat," he proclaimed.

We sang the rest of the commercial together: "There's friendship in the air!"

The sun was low in the sky when Motor Oil, Aspirin, Minivan, and I put on our sand gear and climbed up the stairs of the underground landing pad. There were no barbarians in sight, so we set off across the desert.

"Are you going to tell us your plan now?" Aspirin shouted above the wind.

"Yes, tell us," Motor Oil said. "Are we going to launch a sneak attack on the barbarians?"

"Not exactly," I shouted. "If everything goes according to plan, there won't be any bloodshed at all."

Motor Oil and Aspirin looked baffled. "But how can you defeat the Praxboxian invaders if you don't pound them?" Motor Oil asked.

Minivan tapped his moon-shaped head. "Brain power," he said. "Right, Russell?"

I opened my mouth to answer. That's when we heard it.

Zzzzow! Zzzzow!

"Duck!" I hissed.

We ran behind a spiny chucka plant and threw ourselves down on the sand. We lay there, not moving, not breathing. My heart was pounding so loudly, I was sure the Praxboxians could march right up to me and I wouldn't hear a thing.

Zzzzow!

The sound was getting closer. And then we saw them— three enormous barbarians lumbering through the sand.

Every few steps they let out a ferocious roar and blasted their bazookas into the air.

Motor Oil, Aspirin, Minivan, and I lay there, trembling with fear. But as the barbarians came closer, I saw that they were wearing absolutely no sand gear—no goggles, no hats, no nose protection. Sand was blowing straight into their faces, and they were squinting and holding up their free hands in a pitiful attempt to see where they were going.

That's when I realized the barbarians weren't coming to get us. They hadn't even seen us. They were just wandering aimlessly through the countryside, shooting off their ray guns and hoping they might stumble across some Xarabibblians. As long as we kept out of their way, we'd probably be safe.

I gave my friends a nudge. The barbarians continued stomping, roaring, and blasting. As they came closer, we got to our knees and huddled behind the spiny chucka. Sure enough, they walked right past us. We waited a few seconds, then stood up and ran on.

About twenty minutes—and three barbarian close encounters later—we arrived at a stone hut standing all alone among the spiny chucka. In the distance, the huts of Xarabibblian civilization were vaguely visible.

"This is the power station," Motor Oil said. "At least, we *think* it is. Once, when our power went out, the X-6 scientists sent a worker here. He went inside, and pretty soon the power came on again."

I crouched down and tried opening the tiny door. It was unlocked, which made sense. After all, X-10 was a planet of techno-dweebs. Why would anyone want to break into a power station?

We crawled through the door and stood up. We were in a

big white room with high ceilings and bright electric lights. Everywhere we looked there were bundles of wires, huge transformer boxes, and important-looking switches.

"Wow," Minivan breathed.

"You said it," I agreed. I just wished I knew more about electricity. My grandparents had once bought me one of those little kits that teaches you how to wire a doorbell, but I'd never gotten around to opening it.

"What are we doing here?" Aspirin asked.

"I'm going to redirect all the electricity on the entire planet to the chief's hut," I answered. "At least I'm going to try."

Motor Oil scratched his head. "But why?"

"You'll see," Minivan said. He pointed to a panel of lights and switches on the wall. There was a computer sitting on a table beneath the panel. "Russell, check this out."

I walked over and looked at the panel. It was a map of X-10. A tiny red light marked where each of the Xarabibblian huts stood. Below each light was a number. "Can you show me where the chief lives?" I asked.

Motor Oil stared at the map with a puzzled frown. "He lives in a hut," he said.

"I know that. But can you show me where his hut is on this map?"

"What's a map?" Aspirin asked.

I spent the next fifteen minutes teaching the aliens how to read a map. Finally, Minivan pointed to a red light in the middle of all the other red lights. "The chief's hut is there." He paused. "I think."

I looked at the number below the red light. B-247: I turned on the computer. With Motor Oil's help, I was able to translate the opening menu. One of the options was a file called "Power

141

Flow." I accessed the file and typed in a set of commands to direct the energy output of every windmill on X-10 to the chief's hut. Then I hit ENTER.

The transformers crackled and hummed. The red light marked B-247 began to flash. Then, one by one, the other lights went out.

"You did it!" Minivan shouted.

"Did what?" Aspirin asked blankly.

"I still don't get it," Motor Oil complained.

"I'll explain later," I said. "Let's get moving before the barbarians find us."

We crawled out of the power station and ran across the sand toward the huts. The two suns were setting, but the sky was still glowing with bright pink light. In the distance, I noticed some tall lumps. They rose up from the sand at intervals of about fifty yards all around the outskirts of the city.

"I didn't know trees grew on X-10," I said.

"They don't," Motor Oil answered. "Those are barbarians."

We hid behind a chucka plant and took a closer look. Sure enough, a ring of barbarians was guarding the city, making it impossible to enter or leave. I swallowed hard. Maybe Motor Oil and Aspirin had been right. Maybe there *was* going to be some bloodshed after all—and I had a bad feeling the blood was going to be ours.

"What do we do now?" Minivan asked in a shaky voice.

"Use our brain power," I said, trying to convince myself. I thought hard. "Maybe we can distract them with something."

"Like what?" Aspirin asked.

"Something that would scare them," I said, thinking out loud. "Or something that would excite them."

"You mean like this?" Minivan asked. He unzipped the

pockets of his jogging suit and pulled out a cornucopia of junk food—a bag of pork rinds, a package of beef jerky, five candy bars, a jar of guacamole dip, and a can of Zipsi-Cola.

"Where did you get those?" I asked incredulously.

"We Xarabibblians never go anywhere without our snack food," Motor Oil explained.

"Okay, I've got an idea," I said. "Follow me, and when we meet the barbarians, let me do the talking."

My friends looked at me skeptically. I had a feeling they were beginning to wonder if they'd been wrong to put their faith in me. Actually, I was beginning to wonder that myself. "Let's go," I said, trying to ignore the typhoon that was churning in my stomach.

We stood up and slogged through the sand, heading straight for the nearest barbarian. When we were about fifty feet away, he saw us. *"Alto!"* he roared, pointing his bazooka at us. "Stop!"

It was Quarg! He squinted at us, then let out a low growl. "Quarg's slaves."

"Quarg, buddy, it's great to see you," I said in a cheery voice. Out of the corner of my eye, I could see Motor Oil, Aspirin, and Minivan cowering behind me.

Quarg put one clawlike finger on the trigger of his gun. I gulped and forced myself to keep talking.

"Hey, you're probably wondering why we left in such a hurry, aren't you? Well, there's a very simple explanation. You see, uh . . . a big shipment of snack food was arriving from X-6 and we wanted to be the first in line to get you some." I laughed enthusiastically. "You hungry, pal?"

Quarg nodded warily. "Gimme."

I motioned to Motor Oil, Aspirin, and Minivan. With

trembling hands, they pulled the junk food from their pockets and dropped it at Quarg's feet. As soon as the beast reached down to grab it, I lifted my head and shouted as loud as I could, "Attention barbarians! Quarg has snack food!"

Immediately the barbarians on either side of us came running. "Me want some!" one hollered.

"Ooh, candy!" the other shouted. *"Hitotsu kudasi!"*

"No!" Quarg growled, pushing them away. "Quarg's *een reep chocolade!"*

"You *fryktelig!"* the first barbarian wailed, kicking Quarg in the kneecap. "Gimme!"

Quarg roared and dropped his bazooka. Then he lunged at the nearest barbarian and grabbed him in a headlock. The two fell to the ground, punching and kicking each other. The third barbarian tossed aside his weapon, beat his chest, and then leaped on top.

It was now or never. I reached down and picked up one of the barbarian bazookas. It must have weighed fifty pounds. *"Run!"* I shrieked, and we did.

Chapter 20

zzzow! Zzzzow!

A blast of green light shot past my shoulder. It missed my car by inches and hit a spiny chucka plant. There was a loud crackling sound. Then the chucka exploded in a ball of green flames.

Motor Oil, Aspirin, and Minivan gasped and froze. They stared at the green flames, mesmerized.

I looked over my shoulder. Quarg was lumbering after us. He was about a hundred yards away, but gaining ground fast. The other two barbarians were still rolling in the sand, fighting over the junk food. Two more Praxboxian guards had come over to join the fray.

I looked back at Quarg. He had dropped to his knees and was lifting his bazooka to fire.

"Run!" I shouted at my friends. *"Get going!"* At the sound of my voice, they took off across the sand like race cars on the salt flats.

I struggled to lift the Praxboxian bazooka to my shoulder. Quarg was taking aim. I closed my eyes and pulled the trigger.

Zzzzow!

A blaze of green light exploded out of my gun, half-blinding me. The recoil knocked the bazooka out of my hands and threw me back into the sand. I staggered to my feet, knees knocking and teeth chattering. I thought of looking back to see if I'd hit Quarg, but then I changed my mind. I didn't want to know. All I wanted to do was get out of there.

I left the bazooka lying in the sand and took off. Motor Oil, Aspirin, and Minivan were already zigzagging among the Xarabibblian huts. I caught up with them and together we made our way through the city, eyes peeled for Praxboxians invaders.

It didn't take us long to find some. They were everywhere, wandering among the huts and roaring with dismay because their A-V receivers had died.

"Flashies!" they bellowed. "Want flashies!"

Each time we heard a roar, we crouched behind the nearest hut and waited until the barbarians passed. Then we hightailed it around the next hut.

"Are we almost there?" I asked again and again. My nerves were shot. Hork and his pals were after us, the Praxboxian guards knew we had entered the city, and the streets were crawling with angry barbarians. How much longer could we go on before we were captured and barbecued over crackling green bazooka flames?

"There it is," Motor Oil announced at last, pointing to a stone hut that was at least four times bigger than any other we had passed. "Our beloved chief's hut."

"Uh-oh, I just remembered something," I said. "Didn't you tell me the chief was being held under house arrest?"

Aspirin nodded. "Our great leader told us there are at least ten barbarians guarding him at all times."

I looked around. For once, there were no Praxboxians in

sight. "They must be inside," I said, wishing now that I hadn't left the bazooka in the sand. "Got any more snack food?"

The aliens searched their pockets. Minivan pulled out a bag of peanut-butter-filled pretzels. "I was saving these for later," he said sheepishly.

"Let me have it. Maybe we can distract them long enough to get the projection TV hooked up." I didn't really believe it, but what could I do? We'd come too far and overcome too much to turn back now. Besides, the entire planet was counting on us.

With my heart slamming against my rib cage and my palms damp with sweat, I crouched down and pulled open the chief's stone door. I waited, expecting a barbarian face to appear in the opening, but nothing happened.

My friends and I exchanged a puzzled glance. Minivan shrugged. I took a deep breath, clutched the bag of pretzels to my chest, and crawled through the door. Motor Oil, Aspirin, and Minivan were right behind me.

What I saw made my jaw drop. There were no barbarians. No bazookas. No prison bars or handcuffs or ropes or chains. The room was big and well lit, with off-white walls and plush white carpeting on the floor. Warm air blew through the heating vents and the sweet smell of chocolate filled the air.

In the middle of it all, stretched out on the floor, was the Xarabibblians' beloved chief, gazing at his big-screen projection TV and leisurely nibbling a piece of chocolate cake.

"Honorable Dental Floss!" Minivan cried.

The chief spun around, his blubbery chin quivering. "Motor Oil! Aspirin! Minivan! Earth Citizen Russell! Wha-what are you doing here?"

"Haven't you heard?" Motor Oil said. "Our attack against

147

the barbarians was a failure. We were forced to retreat and hide in the underground landing pad. Then Russell came up with another plan. That's why we're here."

"I thought you were under house arrest," I said. "Where are the barbarian guards?"

"Um . . . er . . . they left," he said. "But first they whipped me mercilessly with their ray guns and warned me not to leave under penalty of death."

I frowned. Dental Floss didn't look like someone who had just been pistol-whipped. In fact, he looked fine.

"We have to hurry," Minivan said. "The streets are filled with blood-thirsty barbarians."

"They are?" Dental Floss said with alarm. "Why?"

"Because Russell turned off all the power," Aspirin explained. "Your A-V receiver is the only one still working."

"What?" Dental Floss cried, leaping to his feet. "You can't do that! The barbarians will kill me—I mean, *us.*"

"Not if my plan works," I said. I ran to the projection box and turned it off. The chief's projection screen went blank.

"What are you doing?" Dental Floss wailed, running after me. His face was red and his chin was wobbling back and forth. He looked like a turkey on Thanksgiving morning.

"Russell, you're upsetting our illustrious leader," Motor Oil said with concern.

"Perhaps we should use someone else's A-V receiver," Aspirin suggested.

"He can't," Minivan said. He turned to me. "Russell, tell the chief your plan."

But there was no time for that now. I grabbed the projection box and crawled out the door of the hut. The extension cord just barely reached.

"Stop!" Dental Floss shouted. "I command you to stop!" He dropped to his knees and began crawling out the door after me. Halfway through, his huge stomach got stuck. He lay there, twisting and thrashing like a beached whale. "Help me!" he groaned. "Help me!"

His cries were answered by a small army of barbarians. It was dark now, but I could hear their roars and see their hulking figures marching toward us.

I was so scared, even my hair was shaking. Frantically, I gazed up through the whirling sand into the sky. The four moons of Xarabibble-10 were glowing brightly. With trembling hands, I pointed the projection box at the largest moon and flipped the ON switch.

For a moment, nothing happened. Then suddenly, a massive blast of power surged through the extension cord and into the box. Sparks shot out the back. Then the grinning face of Chill Cheetah flickered across the face of the moon.

I jumped to my feet and faced the advancing barbarian hordes. At the front of the pack was Hork. He saw me and raised his bazooka.

"Don't shoot!" I shouted, pointing up at the moon. "Look!"

Hork hesitated. He looked. "Flashies!" he bellowed with astonishment. "Way up dere!"

At that moment, Dental Floss managed to squirm through the door. He was followed by Motor Oil, Aspirin, and Minivan. Everyone stared up at the moon.

"Awesome!" Minivan exclaimed.

"Awful!" Dental Floss shrieked. "Turn them off!" He lunged for the extension cord, but Hork lifted his powerful leg and brought his foot down on the chief's arm.

"Kele!" he growled. "Hork like Chill Cheetah."

I turned to him. "What do you think of the big A-V receiver I built in the sky?" I asked.

Hork frowned. "Not big," he said, squinting up through the sand. "Little."

"That's because you're so far away from it," I explained. "The flashies would be really huge if you got close to the receiver."

"Yeah," Minivan added, "and away from all this swirling sand."

The barbarian chief stared up at the moon, transfixed. "Hork want *big* flashies," he growled.

"Hey, I have an idea," I said casually. "What if you flew up there in your spaceship? Then you could get as close as you wanted."

Hork thought it over. He furrowed his hairy brow and scratched his armpits. Then he let out a blood-curdling roar and bellowed, "Bring treats! Start ship! *Je m'en vais!*"

Hork's buddies shoved each other and roared their approval. Then they scattered to spread the word and gather junk food.

"Wait!" Dental Floss cried, grabbing Hork's massive arm. "You can't leave now. Why, you never would have heard of the flashies if it wasn't for me!"

"So?" Hork marched toward the edge of the city with the chief dangling from his bicep. Motor Oil, Aspirin, Minivan, and I jogged after them.

"Fearless leader, what are you saying?" Motor Oil asked with dismay. "Aren't you happy the barbarians are finally leaving?"

Dental Floss didn't bother to answer. "Look, we had a deal," he told Hork. "You can't back out now."

Hork pointed up at the Zipsi-Cola ad that was flickering across the moon. "You got big flashies?" he asked.

150

"Well, no, but—"

Hork flung out his arm and the chief fell to the sand with a thud. He staggered to his feet and ran after Hork, shouting, pleading, and threatening. But the barbarian chief just kept walking through the city, pausing occasionally to gaze up at the moon, throw back his head, and let out a delighted "Har! Har! Har!"

When we reached the other side of the city we saw the Praxboxian ship docked out in the sand. It was a huge, rusted, flowerpot-shaped vehicle with a row of blue lights around the base. Hork kicked the side of the ship with his foot. The lights flashed on and a gangplank descended. He kicked the ship again and a high-pitched siren began to wail.

The siren seemed to act like the Praxboxian version of a dog whistle. Within minutes, dozens upon dozens of barbarians began to arrive. I spotted Mootie, Snorp, and Gwiddle among them. And then I saw Quarg. His hair was singed and he was walking with a limp, but otherwise he seemed to have survived my bazooka blast just fine.

The barbarians were in high spirits. Their arms were filled with junk food that they had looted from the Xarabibblian huts. As they walked, they pointed up at the huge flashies in the sky, chortled, and shoved each other. Then they lumbered up the gangplank after Hork.

Behind them came a group of bewildered Xarabibblians, approaching cautiously. When they saw the Praxboxian invaders getting into their spaceship, they began to whisper excitedly among themselves. Then they spotted Minivan and his parents and hurried over.

"What's happening?" someone asked.

Minivan pointed up at the moon. "The flashies are up

there now," he explained. "The barbarians are leaving to get a better look."

The Xarabibblians looked stunned. Then someone cried, "We're free! We're free!" The crowd began to cheer.

"Give me back my chocolate cake, you hairball!"

At the sound of their chief's voice, the crowd fell silent. Everyone turned to look. The Xarabibblians' beloved leader was running up the gangplank after a barbarian who was carrying a stack of cake boxes. "Give those back!" Dental Floss demanded, stamping his foot. "They're mine! All mine!"

The barbarian with the cake boxes turned and gave the chief a kick right in the middle of his huge stomach. He toppled off the gangplank, fell to the sand, and rolled into a spiny chucka plant.

The Xarabibblians stood and stared, too shocked to move. I glanced over at Motor Oil, Aspirin, and Minivan. I could tell by the sad look on their faces that the truth had finally sunk in. Their beloved leader had sold them down the river for a lifetime supply of chocolate cake.

Then suddenly, the Xarabibblian underground came running out of the darkness. They had looked up at the sky the way I'd told them to do, and now they were coming to see what was going on.

When they saw the barbarians bathed in blue light, tromping onto their spaceship, they let out a whoop of joy. "Russell!" they began to chant. "Russell! Russell! Russell!"

Just then, the last dirty, smelly barbarian disappeared into the ship. The gangplank was pulled up and the engines began to sputter. Dental Floss staggered to his knees and shook his fist, but his words were lost in the roar of the engines. Then, with a foul-smelling blast of black exhaust, the Praxboxian spaceship rose from the sand and flew off into the night sky.

Chapter

21

The Xarabibblians stared into the sky with wonder as the spaceship disappeared into the darkness. I stared, too. I just couldn't believe I'd done it. I, Russell Brinkerhoff, ordinary Earth kid, had driven the Praxboxian invaders from Xarabibble-10. And I'd done it without the so-called superpowers of Captain Spotless and his cartoon cohorts. I'd done it with brain power!

Minivan's voice broke into my thoughts. "Way to go, Russell!" he cried, lifting his hand for a high five.

I slapped his palm and grinned. "I couldn't have done it without you and your folks," I said, and I meant it. During the last few days, Minivan and his parents had begun to change from helpless flashies addicts into self-sufficient human beings—I mean, aliens. I was proud of them.

"Hey," someone suddenly shouted, "isn't that the chief?"

We all turned to see a man dressed in white running toward the huts as fast as his roly-poly legs would take him.

"He's trying to skip out on us!" Minivan cried.

"Get him!" Motor Oil shouted. He and Minivan sprinted across the sand and tackled Dental Floss. Then they grabbed his arms and dragged him back to the waiting crowd.

When the Xarabibblians got a good look at their beloved chief, they gasped. His white jumpsuit was twisted and ripped, his hair was mussed, and there was sand all over his face. He didn't look like a fearless leader any more. He looked like a pouty little boy.

"Okay, let's hear it," I said. "What was the deal you cooked up with the barbarians?"

"What deal?" he shot back. "I don't know what you're talking about."

Aspirin turned to the crowd. "The chief told us he was under house arrest," she shouted. "But when we went to his hut, he was all alone, watching flashies and stuffing his face with chocolate cake."

Aspirin's voice wasn't loud enough to be heard across the whirling sand, but the aliens at the front of the crowd repeated her words to their neighbors. Soon the entire group of Xarabibblians was buzzing with the news.

"We brought Captain Spotless, Lady Bug, Chauncy, and the Stickky Elves from Earth to fight the barbarians," Minivan told the crowd. "We left them in the spaceship. When we returned, the chief was there and our flashies heroes were gone. He let them out."

"That's a lie!" Dental Floss cried indignantly.

But the news was already spreading through the crowd, and the aliens' mood was turning black.

"Earth Citizen Russell hooked up the chief's projection A-V receiver to broadcast the flashies on the moon so that the barbarians would leave our planet," Motor Oil explained.

154

"But the chief tried to unplug it!"

That was the last straw. The aliens gasped as the news spread through the crowd.

"Confess!" someone shouted.

The crowd took up the cry. "Confess!" they chanted, advancing toward the chief. "Confess! Confess!" They formed a circle around him and began poking his fat stomach with their slender fingers.

"Okay, okay, I admit it," Dental Floss finally blurted out. "I met Hork in a pool hall on Xarabibble-6. I was bragging about the trade agreement I had worked out with X-6—sand in exchange for flashies. He was dying to see the flashies, so I made a deal. He could invade our planet if I was treated royally and given all the snack food I could eat."

"But if you were in cahoots with the barbarians," Aspirin demanded, "why did you form the underground and send us to Earth to find Captain Spotless?"

"I never thought you'd succeed," Dental Floss exclaimed. "I didn't think you three could find your way across your hut, let alone across the universe!"

When the crowd heard that, they went ballistic. "String him up!" the normally peace-loving Xarabibblians screamed. "Roast him in potato chip oil!"

Things were turning ugly. Sure, the chief was a low-down weasel, but I didn't want to watch an angry mob turn him into onion dip before my eyes.

"Hold on!" I shouted. "Leave the chief to me. When I'm finished with him, you'll never have to worry about him again."

After the way I'd saved their planet, the Xarabibblians were happy to do anything I said. They quickly calmed down and

155

took up their now-familiar chant. "Russell! Russell! Russell!"

Then slowly, the chant began to change. "Chief Russell!" the throng shouted. "Chief Russell! Chief! Chief! Chief!"

I couldn't believe my ears. Were they saying what I thought they were saying? I looked at Motor Oil. "Stay with us, Russell," he said. "We want you to be our new chief."

Once upon a time, that probably would have been my ultimate fantasy. I mean, sure, I was an introvert and all. But even we shy people have our dreams of power and glory. After all, I was the one who used to fantasize about flying through the sky with Captain Spotless, saving the universe from grit, grime, and evil. Well, this was like a Captain Spotless commercial come to life—only the superhero was *me.*

But after all I'd been through, the idea of living on a planet that worshipped TV commercials and junk food just didn't seem like a dream come true. Instead, all I wanted to do was get back home. I missed my mother and father. I missed my house and my neighborhood. I wanted to see blue sky, feel a warm breeze on my face, and squish my toes into some damp, green grass.

"Thanks," I said, "but no thanks. I'm really flattered by your offer, but I want to go back to my own planet."

"Now?" Aspirin asked sadly.

I nodded. "As soon as possible, please."

For a long moment, no one spoke. That's when I noticed that the wind had died down. For the first time since I'd arrived on X-10, it was almost pleasant. I looked up at the four moons shining brightly above us. A European candy bar commercial was dimly visible flickering across the face of the largest moon. I pictured the barbarians cruising back and forth in their rusty spaceship, staring at the moon like it was an enormous drive-in movie screen.

Minivan must have been thinking the same thing. "Do you think the barbarians will come back?" he asked.

"I doubt it," I said. "Just make sure you keep that projection TV aimed at the moon and don't ever turn it off."

The Xarabibblians thought it over. Their mouths hung open from the strain. Then suddenly something clicked in Motor Oil's brain. "But that will take every bit of electricity we have," he said.

I nodded.

Aspirin looked stunned. "You mean we can't use our A-V receivers ever again?"

"I'm afraid not," I admitted.

The crowd let out a shocked gasp. "No more flashies?" someone cried.

"Well, er . . . no."

The Xarabibblians began to whine and stamp their feet. "We want our flashies!" they wailed. "We want our flashies!"

I stared, barely able to believe my eyes. It was like watching an entire planet of toddlers throw a tantrum. There was only one thing to do.

"Okay, you can have your flashies!" I screamed. When the crowd heard that, they shut up instantly. "But don't forget," I continued, "if I redirect the electricity back to your huts, there won't be enough power to project the flashies across the moon."

"Then the barbarian hordes will come back," Motor Oil pointed out.

"And they'll be mad," Aspirin added.

"That's right," I said. "Now think it over and make your choice."

The Xarabibblians began to argue among themselves in

their native language. I'd never heard so much passionate sneezing and burping in my life. It got so loud, I was afraid a civil war was about to break out.

Suddenly, the ex-chief pulled his arms free from Motor Oil and Minivan's grasp and stepped forward. "Silence!" he shouted at the top of his lungs.

Everyone stopped arguing and turned to look at him. Dental Floss puffed himself up and straightened his soiled jogging suit. "I've got the answer," he said importantly. "If you make me your chief again, I will contact the X-6 scientists and work out a new trade agreement—more sand in return for bigger and more powerful windmills. And that means flashies for everyone!"

The crowd let out an ecstatic cheer. But then Minivan spoke up. "Don't let him fool you," he warned. "He lied to us before and he'll do it again. He might bring back the flashies, but he'll probably charge us twice as many pan-galactic bartering units. And I bet he still won't let us watch the stuff in between the flashies."

"There's stuff in between the flashies?" a member of the underground asked with amazement.

Minivan nodded. "They're called TV shows. I saw them when I was on Earth."

"Xarabibblians don't want to watch those dull stories," the ex-chief said. "They want bright lights, colors, snack food, athletic clothing . . . "

"That stuff is fun," Minivan agreed. "But when you stare at the flashies day in and day out, it numbs your brain. I think we deserve something more."

"Okay, okay," the ex-chief said impatiently, "I won't black out the shows. There, Citizen Minivan. Are you happy now?"

"Actually, no," Minivan answered. "I think we've turned into a planet of A-V addicts. I say we leave our receivers turned off and find some new ways to entertain ourselves."

I gazed at Minivan, absolutely awestruck. I could almost see his brain expanding before my eyes! But the crowd wasn't buying it. There were shouts of "What are you saying?" and "No way!"

"What exactly do you suggest we do?" Dental Floss asked haughtily. "Sit in our huts and watch the wind blow the sand around the way we used to do before the flashies?"

"Of course not," Minivan said. "There are lots of other ways to pass the time. For example, Russell taught me a game called tic-tac-toe. It's really fun."

Then Aspirin stepped forward. "I know something else we can do," she announced. "We can talk."

"Talk?" said the ex-Chief with a snort. "You can't be serious!"

"But I am," she said firmly. "When the barbarian hordes invaded our planet, I thought it was the worst thing that could happen to us. But in a way it was the very best thing, because it brought us together. For the first time in our history, we started talking to each other and working together. We had plans and secrets, hopes and dreams. You have to admit, it was kind of nice."

A murmur swept through the crowd. I saw a lot of heads nodding in agreement.

Then an elderly Xarabibblian with a weathered face spoke up. "But without the flashies *or* the barbarians to unite us, what will we talk about?" she asked. "What will we do?"

"Yeah," a teenaged Xarabibblian piped up. "This planet is a total drag!"

"It doesn't have to be," I said. "There's lots of fun stuff to do together. If you promise you'll throw away your A-V receivers, I'll send back a few things from my planet to help you get started."

"Don't believe him," Dental Floss broke in. "The flashies are the only thing that makes this pathetic planet bearable. You can't live without them and you know it."

"That's where you're wrong," Minivan shot back. He turned to his fellow Xarabibblians. "What do you say? Are you willing to try something new?"

"Yes!" Motor Oil and Aspirin shouted, grabbing the ex-chief so he couldn't escape.

"Yes!" the members of the underground agreed.

"Yes! Yes! Yes!" everyone chanted together.

"All *right!*" I cried triumphantly. "To the underground landing pad!"

"To the underground landing pad!" they echoed. With a smile on my face and the entire population of Xarabibble-10 behind me, I started off across the swirling sand. Now I knew how it felt to be a real hero.

⇒ Chapter ⇐

22

We marched triumphantly through the city and back across the sandy plains. Soon I spotted the dim light of the underground landing pad flickering in the distance. As we walked toward it, Captain Spotless, Chauncy, and the Stickky Elves came running out to meet us.

"Where the heck have you been?" the Captain barked. "We could have dropped dead of old age waiting for you."

"This planet is a dump," Chauncy said with a sniff. "I want to go home."

"Yes, put us back in the TV," the elves begged. "Pretty please with Stickky Adhesive Tape on top?"

That's when it hit me. Lady Bug was missing. She had run off with Hork hours ago and hadn't been seen since. I tried to imagine where she could be. I hadn't seen her board the Praxboxian spaceship with Hork. That meant she could be anywhere—hiding in an abandoned hut, wandering through the sand, maybe even wounded or killed by a barbarian bazooka.

"Poor Lady Bug," I said, wiping a tear from my eye. "The world of TV commercials just won't be the same without her."

"What in tarnation are you blathering about?" Captain Spotless demanded.

"Lady Bug," I sniffed. "She ran off with the barbarian chief and now she's gone forever."

"Pull yourself together." Chauncy chuckled. "She's inside the spaceship. She says she absolutely refuses to set foot on this loathsome planet ever again, and I can't say as I blame her."

I ran to the ladder and looked down. Sure enough, Lady Bug was standing in the doorway of the ship, filing her nails. When she saw me, she glanced up and said, "Well, it's about time you showed up."

"What happened?" I asked. "I thought you were madly in love with Hork."

"I had a brief crush on him, that's all," she replied. "But after I killed off his fleas, I realized we really didn't have much in common. I mean, let's face it. He had lousy manners, and he smelled. So I ditched him and came back here." She put her hands on her hips and tapped her high heel. "What are we waiting for? Let's blow this joint, big boy."

I had to laugh. It looked as if things were back to normal. "Relax," I told her. "I'll be right there."

I turned to face the Xarabibblians. Now that it was time to leave, I felt kind of sad. I was going to miss X-10, and I was especially going to miss the sweet, simple Xarabibblians. I gazed out across the sea of pale blue moon-shaped faces. For the first time in my life, I didn't feel the slightest bit shy or nervous.

"Thank you for inviting me to your planet and making me

feel at home," I called to them. "And most of all, thank you for asking me to be your chief."

The crowd let out a cheer.

"I'm leaving now," I continued, "and I'm taking the flashie heroes, plus Motor Oil, Aspirin, Minivan, and your former chief with me. Captain Spotless and his pals will be put back into the world of flashies. Motor Oil, Aspirin, and Minivan will return with the ship—and with the things you'll need to start your new life."

"Hey, what about me?" Dental Floss demanded.

"That's for me to know and you to find out," I said. I turned to Minivan and his parents. "Let's get going."

Motor Oil, Aspirin, and Minivan grabbed the ex-chief and dragged him down the ladder. Captain Spotless, Chauncy, and the elves went with them.

Now it was just me and the Xarabibblians. "I'll never forget you!" I called. "Good-bye, and good luck!"

"Russell! Russell! Russell!" the crowd roared, lifting their arms to the heavens.

I grinned. I was really going to miss these guys. I waved good-bye, then climbed down the ladder and entered the ship. It didn't take long to program the onboard computer to take us back to Earth. I punched in the proper coordinates, called up the "Take-off Procedures" file, and typed in some commands. Then I hit ENTER.

The ship began to vibrate and hum. Then, with an ear-splitting *whoosh*, we lifted off. I unstrapped my restraining harness and ran to the window.

We were moving so fast that within seconds the Xarabibblians looked like ants on sandpaper. A few more seconds and the entire brown ball that was X-10 was spinning away from us. I could see the planet's two suns rising over the horizons. Then the ship made a hard left and I was looking at stars, stars, and more stars.

We were on our way.

The Earth's sun had just set as we landed in the vacant lot at the end of La Cumbre Drive. I flung open the door of the spaceship and gazed across the empty field to my street. Welcoming lights shimmered in the windows of the houses. I pictured the families inside, finishing up the dinner dishes, talking on the telephone, gathering in the living room to read the paper or watch TV. I sighed. It was only suburbia, but it felt like heaven to me.

"It's good to be home," I whispered, breathing in the smell of the night jasmine.

"What about *my* home?" Captain Spotless demanded, striding up behind me. "The one where every sink is covered with grime and every refrigerator is lined with mold?"

"Where bugs run free," Lady Bug said longingly.

"Where Prime Cut is only a sniff away," Chauncy added.

"And taping is a way of life," the elves chimed in.

"Follow me," I said, climbing out of the ship. While Motor Oil hit the control to turn the ship back into a moving van, I walked across the vacant lot. It felt terrific to step on dirt instead of sand, and to see eucalyptus trees and azalea bushes instead of spiny chucka plants.

The TV characters and I headed up the deserted street to the aliens' house. Motor Oil, Aspirin, and Minivan followed, dragging the ex-chief, who was complaining that Earth didn't look half as bright and colorful as the flashies.

Inside the house, everything was exactly as we'd left it. The

164

smashed TVs sat in the middle of the living room, Captain Spotless's garbage can lay in the corner where he had tossed it, and there was a thin film of dried soapsuds on everything. But most importantly, the computer, the scanner, the VCRs, and the quantum-particle pattern-recognition box were still there, plugged in and ready to go. Now, if I could just find a way to make them work in reverse . . .

I switched on the computer and the box and looked them over. At first, the solution seemed almost too easy to be true. There was a bright red button on the side of the box with the word REVERSE written under it in Xarabibblian. As a test, I set up the software, played a Prime Cut commercial on the VCR, and pushed the button.

Nothing happened.

"Well?" Chauncy muttered, folding his arms across his furry chest. "I don't smell any Prime Cut."

"Mmm," I bluffed, "I must have forgotten a couple of commands. Just let me double-check the software."

I spent the next half hour searching through the software, looking for something that would tell me what I had done wrong. Meanwhile, Captain Spotless and his buddies were growing more and more angry.

"You said you knew how to send us home," Lady Bug pouted.

"It's not a good idea to lie to a hungry dog," Chauncy growled.

"We never would have helped you tape those enormous barbarians if you hadn't threatened to leave us in the real world," said Bert Elf.

The Captain flew in from the kitchen, where he was disinfecting the sink. "We made good on our part of the deal," he warned. "Now it's your turn—or would you rather I scrubbed your brain cells with a Brillo pad?"

"Just give me a few more minutes," I bluffed. "I've almost got this thing figured out."

"You do?" Minivan asked, leaning over the computer screen. Motor Oil and Aspirin came over to join us.

"No," I whispered. I turned to Motor Oil. "I think you'd better call the X-6 scientists and ask for help."

"I would but, uh . . . I've forgotten how to use the radio." He shrugged sheepishly. "It's got buttons and wires and stuff."

I let out an exasperated sigh and glanced over at Dental Floss. He was huddled in the corner with the TV commercial heroes, talking quietly. I had a bad feeling he was trying to stage some kind of mutiny.

Then I had an idea. I checked the wires connecting the TVs, the VCRs, the computer, the scanner, and the box. The one between the computer and the box was a little loose. I pushed it into place and crossed my fingers.

"Okay, let's give it another try," I said. "Elves, let's do you first."

"Oh, boy! Oh, boy!" they squealed, jumping up and down.

"What do we do?" Bo asked.

"Just stand in front of the TVs. Minivan, turn on the Stickky Elves' video."

Minivan hit the PLAY button. As the image of the elves appeared on the TV screen, I flipped the ENGAGE switch on the box. We all held our breath.

Nothing.

The elves, Lady Bug, Chauncy, and Captain Spotless looked at each other. Then they trooped toward the door. The ex-chief followed.

"Hey, where are you going?" I cried.

"Dental Floss made us a deal we couldn't refuse," Lady Bug said over her shoulder. "If we go back to X-10 and help him regain power, he'll set us up in a nice roomy hut with everything we need—like bugs, for example."

"And Prime Cut," Chauncy slobbered.

"Lots of stuff to clean," the Captain added.

"And tape," the elves giggled.

The ex-chief laughed. "So long, Citizens Motor Oil, Aspirin, and Minivan. Hope you enjoy your new life on Earth— because we're taking the ship, and we're not coming back."

"Wait!" Minivan exclaimed suddenly. "I just had an idea. Maybe the pattern-recognition box will work if the flashies heroes stand in the exact same position they were standing in when they came out of the TV."

I gazed at Minivan with awe. "Where did you learn that kind of logical thinking?"

"From you," he said with a grin.

I thought it over. Minivan's idea made sense. If we wanted the box to work in reverse, it had to be able to scan the very same image it had scanned the first time. Then, with luck, it would neutralize the characters' electromagnetic energy and zap their atomic particles back where they came from.

"Let's try it," I urged. "Come back, you guys."

Captain Spotless, Lady Bug, Chauncy, and the elves hesitated at the front door.

"Forget it," the ex-chief said. "That kid doesn't know what he's talking about. Let's blow this planet."

"Just one more try," I said. "If it doesn't work, you're free to go."

Captain Spotless stomped over and shook his fist in my

face. "Send me home or I'll send you to kingdom come!"

Lady Bug, Chauncy, and the elves followed him. Motor Oil, Aspirin, Minivan, and I watched the videotaped commercials to study how the characters had looked when they popped out of the TV. Then we began repositioning them the same way.

"This is a waste of time," Dental Floss said, strolling over to watch us. "It was just luck you managed to make that box work in the first place."

"You think so?" I asked, retrieving Captain Spotless's garbage can from the corner.

He nodded, shaking his chins. "The technology created by the scientists of X-6 is impossibly sophisticated. A mere Earthling can't begin to comprehend it."

"If you're so sure, then I guess you wouldn't mind crouching down inside this garbage can," I said. "I mean, just to prove how wrong I am."

"Oh, so you can send me into the TV, too?" He laughed. "Fat chance."

He was so sure of himself—and so eager to impress the flashies characters—that he climbed into the garbage can. His blubbery body barely fit, but I pushed him down and slammed on the lid. Then Captain Spotless hoisted the can into the air, just the way he did in the Spotless Cleanser commercial.

"It's now or never," I said.

Minivan rewound the videotaped commercials. Then—just as they had done the first time—the aliens hit the PLAY buttons and the four commercials appeared simultaneously on the four TV screens. I flipped the ENGAGE switch on the pattern-recognition box and prayed.

The box began to hum. Chauncy let out an impatient yelp and the elves giggled.

"Don't move!" I warned.

The humming got louder. Captain Spotless's garbage can began to shake as the ex-chief realized he had just made the biggest mistake of his life. I smiled and took one final look at my TV commercial heroes. An instant later there was a flash of blinding light and an ear-piercing blast of white noise.

I squeezed my eyes tight and covered my ears. When I opened them again, Captain Spotless, Lady Bug, Chauncy, the Stickky Elves, *and* the ex-chief were gone.

he aliens and I stared at the empty space in front of the TVs. Then we all jumped to our feet and hugged each other.

"We did it! We did it!" I cried.

"I never thought I'd say this," Motor Oil said, "but I'm glad they're gone. I was getting sick of hearing them complain."

"Do you think the chief is really inside the TV?" Aspirin asked.

"Who cares?" Minivan said. "All that matters is he isn't here."

We let out another whoop of joy and hugged each other again. Then we fell silent. I looked at the aliens and they looked back at me. I knew it was time for my friends to go home.

"Are you sure you don't want to stick around for a few days?" I said. "We could visit Disneyland and take the Universal Studios tour."

Motor Oil shook his head. "Our fellow Xarabibblians are waiting for us. It's our job to teach them how to begin their new lives without the flashies."

"But first, you have to teach us," Minivan said.

"You don't need me," I answered. "You can teach yourselves. But I do have a few things I think will help." I headed for the front door. "Meet me at the ship," I called over my shoulder.

I ran across the lawn to my house. I was so busy thinking about the things I wanted to give the aliens, I totally forgot what was waiting for me. My mom and dad.

"Russell!" my mother shrieked when I walked in the door. She ran at me with her arms outstretched. "My baby!"

"Where in heaven's name have you been?" my father demanded, standing up from the kitchen table.

"Um . . . er . . . with Travis's parents in Oregon," I stammered.

My mother enveloped me in a bear hug and sobbed loudly in my ear. My father ignored her.

"Try again," he said. "When two days passed and we didn't hear from you, we got worried. So we called the Turners this evening. They told us they didn't go to visit Travis at camp, and they had no idea where you were."

My mother pulled herself together and looked at me. "Have you been to the beach?" she asked uncertainly. "You've got sand in your ears."

"Never mind that," my father said. "What I want to know is what you were doing charging four thousand dollars on my credit card?"

I swallowed hard. "How did you know about that?"

"The credit card company called me. Seems they checked

the signature on the slip and noticed it didn't look a bit like mine."

"Where did you get those clothes?" my mother asked. "Have you been jogging?"

I took a deep breath. It was time to come clean. "Mom, Dad, our new neighbors are from outer space. Xarabibble-10 to be exact. Their planet was invaded by barbarians and they needed me to help them zap Captain Spotless out of the TV so he could save them. That's why I used your credit card. We needed a scanner, and a computer that had at least 1.5 gigabytes of—"

"Russell," my father broke in, "do you really expect us to believe that?"

"Tell us the truth," Mom said. "No matter how awful it is, it's better than a lie."

"But this *is* the truth."

"Russell, I'm shocked," Dad said. "You're grounded until you tell me exactly where you've been for the last two days."

"But Dad, you can't ground me!" I cried. "The aliens are getting ready to return to their planet. They're waiting for me to bring them the stuff they need to start their new lives."

"Do you have a fever?" my mother asked, reaching out to feel my forehead.

I pushed her hand away. "Stop it, Mom. This is serious. If you don't believe me, come see for yourself."

My father frowned. "Maybe he had an accident and hit his head. I think he's hallucinating."

"Should I call the doctor?" Mom asked.

"No!" I practically shouted. "Look, I realize you think I've lost my mind. But just wait here two minutes, and I'll prove I haven't. Please?"

My father looked at me skeptically. "Two minutes. Then we're taking you to the emergency room."

I didn't wait to hear more. I ran into my room and quickly gathered up my presents for the aliens. I put them in a shopping bag and hurried back through the living room. "Follow me," I said over my shoulder as I ran out the front door.

"Russell, where are you going?" my mother called.

"Come on, we can't let him out of our sight," my father said.

I sprinted down the sidewalk toward the vacant lot. I could hear my parents scurrying behind me, arguing with each other.

"I told you he was watching too much TV," my mother said. "Something finally snapped."

"Don't be ridiculous," my father shot back. "He just made up that alien baloney. He probably took a bus to Oregon to visit Travis."

"Then why didn't he say that?" my mother demanded.

"Just give me five minutes alone with him and he . . ."

My father's voice trailed off as the vacant lot came into view. The aliens had transformed the moving van back into a spaceship. They were standing in the ship's doorway, their pale blue moon faces glowing in the dim light.

"Oh!" my father gasped. "Oh! Oh!"

"It's not possible," my mother breathed.

"Mom, Dad," I said, walking up to the ship, "I'd like you to meet my friends Motor Oil, Aspirin, and Minivan."

"There are old friends to greet you," Motor Oil sang.

"And new friends to meet you," Aspirin continued.

All three of them joined in on the last line: "So come on in and raise a glass at Murphy's Family Diners."

173

"You're . . . you're . . . you're . . ." my father blathered.

"A-a-a—" my mom stuttered, trying to finish his thought.

"Aliens," I said. "See, I told you. Now, if you'll just give me a minute to say good-bye to my friends, I promise I'll explain everything."

I left Mom and Dad gasping for breath and walked into the ship after Motor Oil, Aspirin, and Minivan. "Here's everything you need to start entertaining yourselves without the flashies," I said. I handed them a rubber ball and a skateboard, a kazoo and a tambourine, a box of crayons, and a package of construction paper.

Finally, I gave them three books. The first was *One Hundred and One Playground Games*. The second was *One Hundred and One Silly Jokes*. The last was *One Hundred and One Stories from Around the World*.

While the aliens stared with wonder at the objects in their hands, I programmed the onboard computer to take them back to Xarabibble-10. Then I gave each of them a hug.

"I'm really going to miss you," I said.

"We'll never forget you, Russell," Aspirin told me.

"We'll come back someday," Motor Oil promised.

"You taught us so much," Minivan said. "Thank you."

"You taught me a lot, too," I answered. "Good-bye, friends."

I gave them one final hug. Then I turned and left the ship. My parents were waiting in the field. I joined them and we watched together as the ship's stairs folded back and the door closed. The ship began to vibrate and hum. Slowly it rose into the air. It hung there for a moment, then whizzed off toward the stars.

Soon the ship was gone, a tiny light among millions of other lights. I turned to my parents. They were staring into the sky with their mouths hanging open. A drop of drool hung on my father's lower lip.

I put my arms around their shoulders. "Let's go home," I said.

As we walked down the street, I gave Mom and Dad a quick rundown of what had happened to me over the last few days. They didn't say much. They just nodded and grunted. I think they were in shock.

When we walked into the house, my parents sat down on the sofa. Dad reached for the remote control and turned on the TV. He and Mom stared blankly at the screen while he channel-surfed. At one point, he paused on a Spotless Cleanser commercial. I did a double take. I was pretty sure I saw ex-chief Dental Floss running across the background, being chased by Princess Poodle.

Then I noticed a postcard sitting on the coffee table. It was from Travis.

Dear Russell, it said, *Even though we can't watch TV, survival camp isn't as bad as I thought it would be. I'm learning how to paddle a canoe, and yesterday I saw a bear. Maybe when I get home, we can go hiking and I'll show you some stuff I learned. Your pal, Travis.*

I smiled and sat down on the sofa. Mom and Dad were still on autopilot, staring at the TV as if nothing had happened. I tried to join them, but I just couldn't get interested. I realized that what I really felt like doing was going outside, maybe lying on my back in the grass and gazing up at the night sky. Only I didn't feel like doing it alone.

"Mom, Dad," I said, "you wanna go outside and check out the constellations? Maybe take a walk around the block?"

Mom and Dad looked at me quizzically. They looked back at the TV, then at me again. Finally, Mom smiled and her eyes seemed to really focus for the first time since she saw the alien spaceship. "That sounds like fun," she said. She took my father's hand and they both stood up.

I opened the front door, took a deep breath, and stepped outside. Then I threw back my head and looked up at the stars. Somewhere up there the people of Xarabibble-10 were about to have their lives changed forever. I grinned. If they were anything like me—and I knew they were—they were going to love it.